A SPELL TO END MAGIC
MOONLIT DREAMS

MONOJIT BANERJEE

BLUEROSE PUBLISHERS
India | U.K.

Copyright © Monojit Banerjee 2024

All rights reserved by author. No part of this publication may be reproduced, stored in a retrieval system or transmitted in any form or by any means, electronic, mechanical, photocopying, recording or otherwise, without the prior permission of the author. Although every precaution has been taken to verify the accuracy of the information contained herein, the publisher assumes no responsibility for any errors or omissions. No liability is assumed for damages that may result from the use of information contained within.

BlueRose Publishers takes no responsibility for any damages, losses, or liabilities that may arise from the use or misuse of the information, products, or services provided in this publication.

For permissions requests or inquiries regarding this publication, please contact:

BLUEROSE PUBLISHERS
www.BlueRoseONE.com
info@bluerosepublishers.com
+91 8882 898 898
+4407342408967

ISBN: 978-93-6452-079-9

Cover design: Shivani
Typesetting: Sagar

First Edition: October 2024

What are dreams made of? The mysteries and wonders of the mind are shaped here; where reality and imagination bend to create their own rules and imagination has a free hand to bend earthly logic.

Some dream of violent ends, some of serene peace. Some are drawn to distant places and some into nearby adventures. Some lead their own story dreaming, while others are thrust into a story of its own. Some wake up rejuvenated to take up the challenges of the day, whereas some never wake up at all....

Prologue

The night had an eerie beauty . There were some clouds in the sky with the moonlight shining down breaking the canopy of the clouds. The passing clouds made the light breaking through erratic, dancing with castedshadows . There, the torches on the walls flickered with the passing cool breeze. The guard over the watch tower looked above in the sky wondering if it was going to rain. If it rained, he will become wet and soggy, for his was an important job and he couldn't leave his post. Even in a calm night like this he needed to be vigilant and careful, for he was the guard over the outermost wall which denoted the boundary of the Sanctamonium, the last known bastion of the human realm. Below him were the great doors, on each side with a huge statue, one of Astolfo and the other of Astaroth, facing off each other, denoting the never-ending conflict between light and darkness. Astolfo was the greatest hero humanity had ever seen, it was said that he created magic and it is his knowledge that has been used through generations. Astaroth on the other hand was darkness reincarnated, he used magic to try to destroy the world and created the "Obscuratus Umbra", the vast area of darkness and shadows the guards were watching over. It was called by different names over the time depending on which Sanctum one belonged to; the Blindspot, the Great Divide or the Eclipse. There were strange creatures lurking inside the darkness and shadows, their origins unknown; no one knew what exactly was inside, except maybe the high ranking Second Division mages and the Magus Knights who had done several excursions into the Blindspot to try a way to destroy the same. It has been more than a thousand years since it came into existence and it divided the world into two; no one knew what was on the other side, except maybe some rumors of life on the other side.

As he shifted his gaze from the sky above towards the darkness ahead, he saw something move. He wasn't sure if it was a trick his eyes were playing on him, he squeezed his eyes to look more clearly. He wasn't mistaken, he could see it clearly now. It was a creature, the size of an overgrown tiger. The hind legs were smaller compared to the forelegs and it had an exoskeleton. It had three horns protruding from the forehead. Its red eyes were visible even from that distance. A kind of black smoke was coming out of its back, making the creature more intimidating. The tail had three splitends with sharp knifelike endings. The guard's heart pounded as he saw the creature prowling, he knew that the situation had turned dire. It was a "Darkseith" and his training had taught him the signal for the same, 3 bells. He started ringing the bell, but he could only hear one ring, though his hand was moving the 2nd and 3rd ring never came.As he turned towards the bell, he could see only the gushes of blood where his hand used to be. He collapsed and as he drifted away into the icy embrace of slumber, he could hear the war cries below from the fellow first division soldiers and the ever present sound from the bell tower every second.

Contents

Chapter 1
The Boy who dreamt to be a Hero 1

Chapter 2
Descend the Stairwell 5

Chapter 3
A Quest for Dominion 11

Chapter 4
Impending Doom 22

Chapter 5
Threshold of the High Council 34

Chapter 6
Moonlit Magic Chamber 44

Chapter 7
The Unfinished Mission 48

Chapter 7
Pandemonium in the Outer Districts 60

Chapter 8
The Shrouded Chamber 70

Chapter 9
Will and Testament 80

Chapter 10
A Plan Sought through ages. 86

Chapter 11
The Condemned Son 90

Chapter 12
Impossible Choices 94

Chapter 13
Call to Arms 104

Chapter 14
The Last Stand 107

Chapter 15
The Everlasting Dawn 120

Chapter 16
The Light beyond the Darkness 128

EPILOGUE 130

Chapter 1

The Boy who dreamt to be a Hero

Sanctamonium, the four walled city stood as a testament of Courage and defiance amidst a desolate landscape scarred by conflicts. With the Central as its capital, there were four concentric walls surrounding the city, it made Central impenetrable to outside forces and Darkseiths. Over the time the Sanctamonium walls also became a testament to the socio economic conditions of the different levels. The inner Sanctum was home to the rich and nobles, with every outer sanctum depleting in value. The outer most circle were the poor with no magical attributes, the castaways and the forgotten. Except for the regiment posted at the outer wall, there was no other evidence of the last sanctum to be a part of the kingdom.

Central was never invaded and the people were so accustomed to ignoring the plight of the outer sanctums that they had forgotten about the Darkseiths. The air in the Central was filled with the smell of exotic spices and the sound of scholarly debates. Trade and industry revolved around the Arcanum and magical items. It housed the esteemed Academy of Magus "Academia Magoram", the dream of every child in the kingdom. It also had the Ministry of magic which looked after all and anything related to magic. The streets were paved with polished stones and glistened under ornate lightings.

As one moved outwards; the scents changed to that of bustling markets and laboring workshops. The Outer districts focused on sustenance farming and basic craftsmanship like blacksmithing and weaving. The second Sanctum was house to the "Academia Militum", which trained first division soldiers in the art of warfare. There were rumors of people selling their young children to the ministry to be made part of the Academia Militum so that later they can serve as soldiers. It ensured handsome salary once the children became soldiers and also a stipend while they were part of the academy. It was a way for the parents to guarantee survival for their children, at least till they became soldiers, and also to cope with their poverty. The First division soldiers had no magical attribute but they were part of the advance forces against Darkseiths, leading them mostly to be fodder against the onslaught. The outermost districts carried an ever present sense of tension; the air filled with smoke and fear, the sounds of scholarly debates replaced by that of hurried footsteps and distant cries of help.

Seraphim Lumenhart, was born in the outer districts to a family of chemists. Chemists were dime a dozen since the country was thrust into mainstream magic. He was mesmerized by the conquests and adventures of Astolfo, the greatest of the greatest heroes, of the exploits of Janus and the Magus Knights. As he navigated the labyrinthine streets of Central with a brisk, purposeful stride, his cloak, the hue of twilight shadows, rippled behind him like a banner caught in a relentless wind. The city was awake with the murmurs of dawn, vendors crying out their wares, waking the town to the first trades of the day. Stood before him were the spires of Academia Magoram, its edifice towering over the surrounding structures. Behind him he could hear the sound of the bell tower denoting every second. It had been three years since he was chosen to be a Magus, the entrance exam, taken at just fifteen years old, had determined Seraphim's fate as a mage.

As Seraphim entered the grand courtyard which was bathed in the morning sun, casting a warm glow over the ancient stone buildings and lush green gardens, his eyes lingered on the intricate carvings and statues that adorned the walls, symbols of the powerful magic that was taught within. The air was filled with the sweet scent of blooming flowers and the slight hint of burning incense. The stone pathway was cool beneath his feet as he walked toward the center, the smoothness of the stones and the softness of the grass provided a familiar sensation.

He crossed the Courtyard to enter the halls, each step falling on the stones which stood testament to the determination of countless mages before him to master the secrets of "Magia Somnia", the magic drawn from weaving the energy of dreams. Seraphim read the phrase above the oak doors outside his class, "Clarior lux Obscurior Umbra" — "the brighter the light, the darker the shadow". He acknowledged this with a solemn expression, understanding the gravity of the warning. He would use his knowledge with honor, intellect, and compassion guiding him in defense of all he held dear. With a final glance at the engraving, Seraphim stepped into the classroom, ready to embrace the arcane wisdom that awaited him and to be a step closer to joining the rank of mages.

Chapter 2

Descend the Stairwell

The musty air clung heavily to their lungs as Seraphim Lumenhart, Rayburn Wilder, and Tomoe Shinsei descended the long stairwell, the narrow steps spiraling into the bowels of the Academy of Magus. The flickering torches cast elongated shadows on the walls as if spirits of the past watched their decent.

The three were unusual friends, brought together by their common purpose and a hand of fate. Rayburn Wilder was the adopted son of Janus, the greatest Mage of the time. He was the leader of the Magus Knights and belonged to a long line of mages in the family. As the story goes, one day when Janus and his eldest son Tiberius, were visiting the Outer Sanctum for a mission, a scrawny little boy ran towards their convoy and tried to hide amidst them. He was being followed by some bullies and he showed signs of struggle. Though beaten his eyes shone bright with fervor and determination. Janus with one look knew that Rayburn was built for greatness and saw the fire within him. He was an orphan and so Janus adopted him and brought him home. He gave him not only his name but a life where he could live with dignity and command the respect of his fellow members. There was no one who wore the emblem of the "Gravestone" family more proudly than Rayburn. Janus was not just his father, but his mentor and a God reincarnated.

The only friend Rayburn ever had was Tomoe. His quiet demeanor and measured words mostly kept people at bay, maybe only Tomoe knew who Rayburn actually was. She was also the voice of reason between Rayburn and Seraphim. She was a beauty to behold, with the fierceness of a warrior. Her demeanor, though always calm and composed, was akin to fire that could burn all. She came from a long line of Mages as well, born and brought up in the central. Her robes carried the Shinsei family crest, one of the richest and influential mage families in Central. They always wanted her to become a mage and join the Ministry following the footsteps of the forefathers, but she was a warrior at heart and had her heart set to join the Magus Knights. Tomoe and Rayburn grew up together as family friends and over time they became closest confidants.

Seraphim,unlike the duo, was upfront and believed in speaking his mind. He was a go getter, often acting before thinking. He believed in making friends and had a knack to help people around, sometimes even against their will. He and Rayburn started off disliking each other, each trying to outdo the other in their classes. Their rivalry was well known among the students, Seraphim with natural talent to understand and pickup magical skills and Rayburn with the knowledge about the intricacies of magic very few possessed. Over the first year, through numerous interactions, most of which were about between Seraphim and Rayburn, and Tomoe brokering peace, the trio started respecting each other for their values.

It was Tomoe who noticed the absence of Seraphim in the class and the presence of some people from the Ministry of Magic in the Academy. The attacks on the Outer Sanctums and skirmishes with the Darkseiths were common and not a popular topic to be discussed in the capital except for the news articles which were circulated every morning; today was one of such days and the area of the attack seemed familiar to her. Later she along with Rayburn found Seraphim sitting on one of the tall spires of the Academy alone deep in thought and with fire in his eyes. As their eyes met, the emotions he had been holding in bay broke all barriers and tears rolled out from his eyes. Rayburn embraced Seraphim and the only words that came out of him were "We have to destroy the Blindspot, those creatures killed my dad". Rayburn and Tomoe embraced him tighter, none alien to the feeling of loss, and through that embrace they became more than friends.

Almost a year and a half had passed since they joined the academy when one day, while exploring the older sections of the library, Tomoe discovered the stairwell which led to an even older section with scrolls and books from a forgotten era. Since then it had become a frequent visit for the three to the hidden chamber to unravel the mysteries kept within though they decided not to divulge the secret to anyone else and more importantly not to explore the locked chamber on the farther corner.

Today they ventured back into the chamber. The staircase led to a grand archway, an entrance fit for a kingdom's treasure vault which led to the vault. The vastness of the chamber was hidden in darkness, only lit by the torches carried by the group. What little light there was, glimmered off surfaces cluttered with artifacts of undeniable antiquity, and rows of shelves burdened with texts.

"Look for anything that speaks of dreams, connection to Multiverse or anything out of the ordinary." Seraphim instructed, his voice echoing through the silence, his fingers tracing the leather bounds of the books, which spoke of long forgotten tales.

"Here!" Tomoe called out, her fingers brushing over a scroll that shimmered with a subtle enchantment. She motioned the others closer, her discovery casting a spell of urgency upon them.

"Could this be it?" Rayburn asked, leaning in to inspect the delicate inscriptions. The symbols were intricate, weaving together the languages of High Magic with the more elusive script of the multiverse's fabric.

"Only one way to find out," Seraphim said, his eyes alight with the thrill of the chase. He joined Tomoe, dissecting the patterns and sigils that promised answers to the questions they had scarcely dared to ask.

Together, they poured over the text, the chamber echoing with the sounds of turning pages and hushed revelations. Each word they deciphered brought them closer to understanding the enigma of the Great Divide or Blindspot—a phenomenon as elusive as the dreams from which Sanctamonium's magic was born.

"Darkness and light, woven together in a tapestry of power," Seraphim murmured, tracing a line of ancient text. "Astolfo Starlight and Astaroth Darkstorm, the heroes of old who knew its secrets."

"Astolfo Starlight, his name is woven into the text like a golden thread." His finger rested upon an elaborate glyph that shimmered with light.

"Indeed," Tomoe added, her gaze flitting across the page. "The narrative unfolds like a tapestry of celestial design; Astolfo, the dream weaver who stood sentinel over our realm."

Their eyes moved in unison, absorbing the tale of valor and sacrifice penned by hands from a millennium ago. It chronicled Astolfo's rise, a paragon of virtue among mages, his soul intertwined with the essence of dream magic. His quest to shield Sanctamonium from Astaroth's enveloping shadow had been one of both splendor and sorrow.

"See here," Rayburn said, pointing to a passage where the ink itself seemed to mourn. "The creation of the Obscuratus Umbra it fractured the dreamscape, sowed seeds of chaos where once there was order."

"The Great Divide," Seraphim whispered his voice barely louder than the rustle of ancient pages. "It was a nexus, an anchor for dream magic that sprawls across the multiverse."

Astolfo's Magic Somnia left cracks within the cosmos. And through those cracks..."

"Astaroth's darkness seeped in," Tomoe finished, her graceful composure belying the gravity of her words.

"Here," Seraphim whispered, the word slicing through the hushed chamber like a blade. "It speaks of a nexus, a focal point where dream energy converges—where the Blindspot can be unwoven."

Seraphim met Rayburn's storm-filled gaze, then Tomoe's resolute stare. In that shared glance, words were redundant; their commitment was absolute. They stood united, three beacons of light amidst encroaching darkness, each bearing the mantle of protector, scholar, and warrior.

Seraphim closed the manuscript with care, his blue eyes alight with steely determination. With the manuscript secured beneath Seraphim's arm, they turned to face the chamber's exit. The light of their resolve pierced the darkness that sought to encroach upon their sanctified ground. They were about to embark on more than a mission; it was a crucible that would forge their destinies and reveal the true mettle of their spirits.

Chapter 3

A Quest for Dominion

Seraphim's voice echoed within the dimly lit study where he gathered with Tomoe and Rayburn.

"We cannot ignore the plight of the outer districts, not with the knowledge we possess. We must share what we know and devise a strategy with the Magus Knights".

"The only thing that will achieve is getting yourself expelled, the Magus knights will never listen to a bunch of students, and why should they? Also how will you explain the manuscript and the chamber, even we don't know exactly what the script means." chimed Tomoe.

Rayburn Wilder, standing opposite Seraphim, pressed his hands onto the ancient oak table. "They have increased patrols, Seraphim, But these creatures... they're elusive, striking where we least expect."

As the three deliberated, Seraphim's attention was drawn to another hushed conversation from a nearby table in the study. Two senior mages, robed in the deep blues of the Academy, spoke in tones heavy with secrecy.

"Indeed", the Blindspot has remained untouched since the age of Astolfo. The Magus knights have not been able to gain any ground."

"Yes, and the recent attacks are starting to leave their mark on central as well."

As the senior mages left the study, Seraphim couldn't help but notice that within the Central the talks of the Blindspot were not elusive anymore. The dangers posed by the Darkseiths didn't seem a distant threat, and the whispers of the tales echoed in every corner.

He knew that it is the time to act. He needed a way to pass on the information and be a part of the efforts of the magus Knights.

"Selene Moonshadow," he whispered the name as if it were an incantation capable of unlocking the secrets of the cosmos itself.

Selene was a member of the High Council, but she stayed at the Academy and acted as the guest faculty. She had caught his potential in the first year itself.His thirst for knowledge and resolve often brought him to her doors for guidance. He had told her about the chamber and she had kept it to herself, instilling a trust in Seraphim.

With the darkness of the night covering Seraphim as a cloak, he navigated through the corridors of the Academy towards the chamber of Selene. His mind kept going back to their first encounter and his first lecture in the Academy.

Miss Daisy Donel was in her early thirties. Her face was kind but her demeanor strict. She took her place in front of the teacher's chair, wrote her name on the board and turned around glancing at the class, her eyes looking deep.

"Why do you want to learn magic?"

A few hands shot up in the class.

"Ok, before that, do you know the origin of magic, why are we able to conjure spells and why do only a few uses or connects to a higher power?"

The hands came down one by one and all eyes fell on Miss Daisy.

She smiled, "Let's dive into the world of the unknown and unravel its secrets, maybe that will give you a bit more clarity as to why you want to be a magus."

When she knew she had the undivided attention of the class, she started to speak again.

"Magic and science are close sisters. To understand magic you have to understand the science behind it, because you cannot break the laws and consider magic to be an all-powerful tool. Since the dawn of mankind, people have looked up and gazed at the stars imagining a world beyond and trying to understand our existence and to put it in perspective. Scholars predicted the future or weather based on the movement of the stars and planets; they even tried to predict the nature and characteristics of a person by understanding the alignment at the time of their birth. Astronomy is a science that has been studied since ages.

She continued, "But does that explain the existence of magic, not in its entirety. The other aspect to complete the picture somewhat lies in our brains and our minds. Every one of us dreams when we sleep; many scholars and scientists have tried to find the meanings. Some see violent dreams whereas others have peaceful ones; some see events that have never happened to them, but yet feel real, some don't even remember what they dreamed about. Over time, scholars have argued that dreams are our mind's way to rationalize whatever happens in our daily life, our subconscious in work. After a lot of research, scholars have some inclination that apparently, our dreams are a gateway to a realm that connects our world to other worlds. Multiverse has been a topic of much discussion and debate over the recent years, and though proven in theory; there is much to be covered in the field.Its biggest proof of concept lies perhaps in our dreams".

So now the question that might come to your mind is that almost everyone dreams, and planets and stars exist for everyone, so if magic has origins in Astronomy and dreams, shouldn't everyone be able to use magic? Well, that's where the lines get a bit blurred and we use the term magic as the exact science cannot be explained. Otherwise, we might have been able to call it alchemy. Not everyone who dreams can connect to the higher realm, and even among people who can, some can only do so during specific planet alignments. That's why not all can use magic.

The test you guys had at the time of the entrance was to check if you can connect to the realm; though not an exact science, we can test for the same. The headgear does help to amplify the connection by putting you in a deeper state of sleep, and yes, the deeper you sleep, the better the connection. It is theorized that, as per the assumptions in multiverse theory, there are other planets with the existence of life, and that dreams can connect between these existences and magic users can draw from that power. Over the next three years, we will try to teach you how to connect and draw that power, if you can, while being conscious and using the same to perform miracles. As people say, two brains are better than one."

With that, Miss Donel paused for the information to settle in. The class was in silence, trying to absorb the lecture and understand the implications.

Miss Donel continued, "Normally, the connection is created while you sleep, so how do you connect when awake? For that, we have to use a "Transmogrification Circle" commonly called a "Transmutation Circle"— a different name used by scholars and Magus. Initially the number of people who could use magic were even less, it was Astolfo who created Transmutation circles a thousand year ago which has increased the users of magic and also standardized the uses. As the name suggests, they change the property of the energy drawn to a usable energy which can be used for many purposes. It's like we have coal and water, but we need a steam engine that helps to convert that thermal energy to be used to run machines, a transmutation circle basically does the same, though the optics are vastly different. We cannot use the energy in nature to transmute into an energy we can use as human beings; we have machines for that.Basically thermal, hydro plants use the energy readily present in nature.

A transmutation circle has three parts:

1. The Circle: It depicts the connection between everything and the natural flow. The basic principle was transformation; energy cannot be created nor destroyed, only transformed.

2. The Energy: To transform, energy was first drawn and absorbed and later changed to be used in the fashion the user wanted, depending on what the desired outcome was. For an energy attack like a fire attack, energy has to be released, for defensive uses, like diffusing a magical attack, the energy has to be absorbed.

3. The Gate: It is the valve for drawing and releasing the energy. The bigger the gate, the more power you can draw, and the more effect it has on the body. If you draw less than what was required, the magic won't be successful, and if it's more, it will backfire.

But this is just scratching the surface. We are trying to change mental energy to physical energy, although we are successful in doing so, still, there is a lot to be understood; thus, we use the term "Magic".

Maybe it was due to his training as a chemist, but Seraphim was able to visualize the Transmutation circle in his mind.

Miss Donel asked for a volunteer to try to replicate one and Seraphim was the first to raise his hand. The Circle was incomplete as it was only for demonstration, but Seraphim was able to decipher the circle and also point out how to complete the same.

Selene was sitting at the back of the class, like she did quite often; she liked to see the excitement in the faces of the young ones eager to take up the challenges of the world. Seraphim caught her eye when he completed the circle and was able to draw a trinket of magic from the transmutation circle to create a small gush of wind within the closed class.

A cold breeze brought Seraphim back to the present. At the threshold of Selene's study, the door swung open with a silent consent that only magic could grant. There, amidst tomes that whispered tales of eons past, stood the High Council Member. Silver hair cascading like moonlit water, her piercing grey eyes met his with an intensity that mirrored the gravity of his quest.

"Seraphim Lumenhart," Selene greeted her voice the soothing calm before the storm. "Another quest into the chamber I presume, further tales of the Blindspot you seek?"

"Indeed, Lady Moonshadow," he replied, "I must understand the nexus between dream magic and the Blindspot."

Selene regarded him with a gaze that transcended mere sight. Her nod was slow and deliberate.

"Let's meet up tomorrow after your classes. Bring your friends along too; I am sure they are as eager as you, though maybe not so bold". Seraphim didn't expect to receive help so soon; he was at a loss of words at the invite. He handed over the manuscript and gave a nod and Selene closed the door to her chambers. Standing in the moonlit corridor, Seraphim started to see a path forward, forged by his own hands.

Next day the trio knocked on the huge oak doors of the chamber. Rayburn hadn't taken the message well, he was furious that Seraphim didn't consult before handing over the manuscript. If the information of their late night adventures reached Janus, they would surely in trouble. Along with everything else Janus was always a strict with rules. Tomoe as usual brokered peace and they had all agreed to take decisions together going forward.

Selene had a way with her words; her demeanor spoke of her experience. She was herself a researcher and was always calm and poised in her explanations. She made explanations of the arcane a breathtaking story unfolding in real time.

"The manuscript you found is of utmost importance and I have presented it to the High Council and Magus Knights. Rest assured, I have kept your names out of the conversation. In return, I will help you with the mastery of advanced magic, which would have taken years of practice to master otherwise."

"Behold, young mages," Selene intoned, "the realm of dreams is the crucible where reality is tempered. It is within this ethereal forge that the Blindspot was born—a blemish upon the fabric of existence, where the laws of magic fray."

"Your quest," Selene continued, her grey eyes piercing the gathering shadows, "is to harness that which lies dormant within you. Dream magic is the key. Connect to the higher realm in slumber, draw upon its power, to understand what you seek first, you have to know the depths of your power."

"Transmutation circles serve as guides, as crutches. To cast spells without them requires not only precision but also an intimate dance with the multiverse—a connection so profound that your very dreams weave the fabric of reality."

"Visualize and your magic will speak to you, just like your dreams do. Not all magicians are same and nor are their magic, look within yourself, know your mind, you are trying to understand dreams and for that you need to understand yourself, dive deeper within yourself."

For the next many days the trio deepened their understanding of magic under the tutelage of Selene, trying to draw out their magic.

Using Magic without transmutation circles though possible in theory, wasn't a common practice. One had to imagine the circle with precision in one's mind to draw the energy, and more often than not, people failed spectacularly. The Warlocks who used magical weapons had transmutation circles drawn on them, similar to the mages who used staffs or wands. The weapons, staffs, and wands, are specific to the individual using them.

Seraphim closed his eyes, as he envisioned the flow of magic, he could see the flow of the wind, serene and cool, yet sharp and furious. To him magic was like the flow of the wind, although one cannot see it, it was all around him.

Rayburn's brow furrowed as he envisioned the ebb and flow of water, the lifeblood of creation. He could envision the flow between rivers and streams, all flowing into the deep oceans.

Tomoe's fierce determination ignited her inner vision, conjuring images of fire dancing at her command. Magic for her was fierce, capable of giving light and warmth, but capable of turning everything to ash if trifled with.

Selene urged, her tone unwavering. "Trust in your abilities. The cosmos does not yield its secrets to the fainthearted.Try Again."

Finally after a month, one day, Selene gathered them, "Let the legends remind you," Selene intoned, her grey eyes alight with the fire of conviction, "that the path to greatness is paved with relentless pursuit. Rise, my apprentices, and embrace your destinies."

"Each has a different magical attribute, the way the magic calls to one is special and unique. You, Seraphim Lumenhart, will learn to dance with the wind—to command it with the finesse of a poet and the precision of a scholar. Your task is to bend the gales without breaking them, to master the subtlety of breezes and the fury of storms alike."

Seraphim nodded, his piercing blue eyes reflecting a storm of determination. The air around him seemed to quiver in anticipation, sensing the will of its soon-to-be master.

Rayburn's muscles tensed as Selene directed her attention to him next. "Rayburn, water is the essence of life—yielding yet persistent, calm yet capable of great destruction. Your charge is to refine your control over this element, to shape it with both gentleness and strength, until it heeds your call as naturally as the tides obey the moon."

He closed his eyes, envisioning the ebb and flow of mighty rivers, feeling the cool embrace of the water's spirit calling to him.

Finally, Tomoe met Selene's gaze, the flicker of flames reflected in her eyes. "And you, Tomoe, must forge a bond with fire that is unbreakable. Kindle its warmth, harness its wrath. Strengthen your connection until it becomes an extension of your very soul."

"Go now," Selene commanded, her presence an undeniable force in the vast chamber. "Harness the elements; let them resonate with your spirits. Push beyond what you believe possible."

Chapter 4

Impending Doom

The Ministry of Magic was built of glass and stone. It was the symbol of magical authority within Sanctamonium and Central. It was a bureaucratic institution which ran along with the Magus Knights to manage the affairs of the state and anything related to magic. Within its grand hall, deliberations were going on as the current issue divided the ministers. Janus and Selene had presented the Manuscript found by Seraphim, Rayburn and Tomoe to the Ministry. The High council was of the opinion that a reconnaissance force should be sent into the Blindspot, into a specific area called the "Eclipse". It was the origin of the Blindspot as per the manuscript. It was where Astolfo had his last stand against Astaroth and the fabric of dreamspace was cracked enough for the Blindspot to originate. Janus and the Magus Knights were against the idea as it would mean loss of lives of good mages.

"And who do you choose for this mission? Surely you would inform them that it's a suicide mission" remarked Janus.

"Not necessarily," replied Mathew, one of the leading members of the high council, "and losses of lives is not new to us. We have to make sacrifices for the greater good. We will ask for volunteers, no doubt there are still a few brave souls among the Magus Knights."

Janus looked at Mathew with bloodshot eyes at the comment, "Yes, the brave souls are all within the Ministry, who are eager to send young souls to their deaths."

Selene who was quite so far spoke up "Perhaps, we should find out more information before launching a mission. Caution doesn't imply cowardice."

"The discovery of the Manuscipt is a new grain of knowledge which came after eons" interjected Mathew, "I am ready to believe that you found it during your casual stroll within the academy but can you provide a timeline by when we will receive another such vital document?"

Every one fell silent. Selene knew that disclosing the origin of the discovery will lead to expulsion of the students. She herself had gone through the chamber but wasn't able to find anything tied to the Blindspot, the scripts and books were all related to magic and history.

"Seems it's decided then, I believe the best of the Magus Knights are already present here, do we have a volunteer to lead the mission?"

As everyone looked around for a hand to be raised, a voice boomed across the hall, "I will".

Janus, who had been looking at Mathew with rage in his eyes, heard the familiar voice and turned around to see

Tiberius stepping up. His jaw immediately tightened and with measured tone he addressed Tiberius. "What is the meaning of this? Do you not agree in the futility of this mission? Does my and Satori's logic not make sense to you?"

"It does, but if this has even the slightest chance of being a success, you know I will have to be a part of it" replied Tiberius with calm in his voice which diffused the tension in the room.

Tiberius was one of the best Mages, second maybe only to Janus and Satori. Though young, he had the wisdom of a matured Mage and his use of magic was exceptional. His magical aptitude was fire, but unlike most, his flames were blue. His sword the "Gleaming Sorrow" had become a beacon of hope among the citizens as whenever the blue Mage rode out and the Sword burnt bright.It spelled doom for the Darkseiths and hope for the people. He regularly volunteered to patrol the Outer districts and helped the people from the outer Sanctums even in small chores where he could. It was in one of these patrols he and Janus found Rayburn. He was the favorite son of Sanctamonium and most probably in line to lead the Magus Knights.

"We are all desperate to put an end to the Blindspot; we have started to take the losses granted now. The Outer Sanctums are attacked and lives are lost but we here in Central don't even have a memorial for them. We have accepted the losses of lives as regular part of life and the news doesn't even bother us. Is that the world we want to keep living in? If this mission can produce a ray of hope to destroy that darkness, the darkness not just beyond the walls but the one that has started to make home within our very hearts, I would gladly lead it. I will have my team ready by nightfall and we can leave in the dark of night".

The Hall fell silent; the truth spoken by Tiberius wasn't one that was unknown to the Ministry or the Magus Knights.

Outside the hall, Janus again implored Tiberius. "Son, you know your chances. Eclipse is at the heart of the Blindspot, there is a reason we do not send out Mages for mission there. There has been none who returned from there, alive or not. Also we do not know what you will find there, if anything the risks far outweigh the probable rewards."

"We are not going to defy the Ministry now, you know that. You stand for the law of the land, and Mages do work in accordance to the Ministry. Who would you rather send on this mission, who would you choose to lead this mission, give me an alternate and I would back down."

Janus knew there was no one else more capable than Tiberius.

"Now, let me take my leave and meet my brother before leaving". Tiberius left with a usual reassuring smile on his face.

For Rayburn, Tomoe and Seraphim the visits of Tiberius were always a welcome one. He was not just Rayburns big brother but had become the brother to all three.

"Hand over your sword, how long are you going to carry that thing. Its time it found its real master," joked Rayburn. Rayburn was different around him, he was happy and jovial, a side which was rarely seen in him.

"Maybe someday, first learn to hold a sword properly. More importantly I heard that you guys found a Manuscript with secrets of the Blindspot. It has vital information,so on behalf of the Magus Knights,I thank you. But I hope Father doesn't find out, or you guys will be in trouble," winked Tiberius.

"It was Tomoe who found it, we were just standing around," remarked Seraphim.

"Oh, it was Tomoe is it? Then it's all right, my sweet sister can't be wrong and can't do anything wrong. I thank you Tomoe" said Tiberius with a glint of mischief in his eyes.

Tomoe in return couldn't help but blush.

"Anyways I will take my leave, I have a minor mission tonight, so just wanted to meet my favorite trio before leaving."

As Seraphim, Rayburn and Tomoe watched Tiberius leave, their fire inside shone even brighter. They couldn't wait to be part of the ranks of the Magus Knights and be able to ride out to fight the darkness soon.

The Grand Hall was silent; the only sound was the heavy breathing of Janus. The usually calm Leader of the Magus Knight was distraught, his eyes a storm of despair and anger. It seemed it will engulf everyone around. It had been a week since Tiberius had left for Eclipse with five of his best Mages. Today his wounded and shattered body was found just outside the wall, the rest of the comrades lost within the Blindspot.

"We have to put an end to this; we need to put an end to the Blindspot". Janus's voice was a deep rumble, carrying the weight of the mountains.

The Ministers and other Knights wanted the same, the entire Sanctamonium wanted the same, but there was no path open to achieve the goal. Janus sat on his chair, his hand on his forehead, his face barely visible through the thick of his hair.

"Easier said than done," came a soft murmur from amongst the people gathered.

Without raising his face, Janus echoed though the chamber "Selene".

Selene stood up at attention as if on cue. "The mission wasn't a total failure. Tiberius came back with a parchment with information, hidden within the sheath of his sword. He discovered a nexus between the planets and the Blindspot. We are confident that on certain astronomical events the Blindspot falls weak and is susceptible to attacks. From our understanding, the darkness is created because of the cracks in the dreamspace and there is a way to reverse it or so to say control it. As per my calculations the optimal alignment of the planets would be in four months on the ides of March."

"Even then this is all theory, we have already lost some of our best mages, and how do we plan to launch a full attack in four months with just theories? If we fail we will have no defenses left against the next attack from the Darkseiths."

"Then we will not fail, I will make sure we won't fail", rumbled Janus.

"But...." The voice stopped in its track as Janus raised his head to look at the minister. His eyes bore deep into the minister and he felt like his legs started to tremble. It was as if the entire being of Janus had found a point to focus its anger and anyone who came in between would be sharing in his wrath.

No one else spoke as Janus stood up and walked out. Satori his second in command joined Janus.

"It's time.." Satori nodded to his mentors remark and left to start his preparations.

Back at the Academy, it was time for the final exams for third year. It was another three years before the students would become a full fledged Knight. Rumors of the secret training of the trio already spread within the campus and they were seen with either jealousy or with contempt. Seraphim was bothered by the looks as he was accustomed to people liking him. Rayburn and Tomoe on the other hand didn't pay any heed to the others. They were busy studying the different transmutation circles when a messenger came into the study searching for Rayburn. He was informed that Janus had summoned him and he rushed out at once, leaving Tomoe and Seraphim behind.

Leandra seeing that Rayburn was away took the opportunity to talk to Seraphim and Tomoe. She was from the Central, a senior and was very popular in the Academy.

"How do you guys hang around Rayburn, he always has a dark aura around him, always serious. You highborn mages with your family crests and your swords hanging around even before you become mages; you can be a bit relaxed as well."

Seraphim glanced at Tomoe as the comment was directed at her; her smile put him at ease.

"Anyways I heard you guys are having special training with Selene, that's a good way to earn extra marks, you should get all the help you can while at the Academy."

"The training is not aimed to get extra credits", interjected Seraphim but before he could finish his sentence Leandra chimed in.

"So the rumors are true, you aim at conquering the Blindspot, you do know that scores of mages have tried and failed. Even the Magus Knights have not made any headway. If Selene was capable enough to defeat the Darkseiths, she would have already. Don't you think it's a wasted effort?"

The words hung in the air for some time. Seraphim hadn't considered the fact that even though gifted, Selene wasn't able to conquer the Blindspot; she wasn't even part of the Magus Knights and was a council member in the Ministry of Magic.

"To reach the destination one must travel on the road, the people who walk ahead of you provide a clearer path and the ones you pass along the way have their insights and experiences, none is less valuable than the other". Tomoe's words broke the silence; her wisdom was always beyond her age. Seraphim felt at ease to have Tomoe beside him. She was the voice of reason, her council always invaluable.

Leandra smiled in return, "well said and I cannot agree more. Well there are others who share the same passion and have the same goals, in time you guys will need companions along the way, remember that nothing brings people together more than a shared objective and a common enemy."

"You are born in central, do you even care about the plight of the Outer Districts?" asked Seraphim.

"Sanctamonium is Sanctamonium, the sky above us is the sky and the land below is the land, walls in between doesn't change that. If today we ignore the plight of our neighbors', tomorrow that plight will surely visit us. Divide and conquer is the motto of the Politicians, we are just students". Whenever she spoke she had this twinkle in her eyes and a smile on her face. "Will introduce you to some of my friends someday, but for now let's call it a night". With that Leandra took her leave, Seraphim and Tomoe sat there wondering how to react to her invite.

The next morning everyone was woken up early as the morning bell for announcement rang over the loud speakers. Seraphim woke and sat up straight unable to find Rayburn beside him. It was cloudy outside, reflecting the gloom of the announcement. There had been a tragedy, five of the best Mages were considered dead while on a mission to the Blindspot. Tiberius was the only confirmed loss as his body was discovered. Everyone was to be gathered in the "Field of the fallen heroes" to bid the heroes a final farewell.

It was as if the entire City was gathered in the Field, all in their black robes. The sky was also about to cry contemplating the loss. The Loss of Tiberius was felt by everyone; he was dear to everyone, the loved son of Sanctamonium. Janus was kneeling in front of the Monument that represented the fallen heroes. Only the sound of thunder broke the heavy wall of silence which fell on the Field.

Rayburn and Tomoe were beside Janus. Tomoe had controlled herself enough, she felt weak in her knees and faltered down, tears rolling down her cheeks.

"We donot mourn our heroes", came the rumbling voice of Janus, "We accept their sacrifice and feel grateful that we could have birth such heroes. We are not to shed tears, but make these sacrifices etch its story in our hearts. We do not mourn but we use those feelings to fuel the fire inside."

Janus stood up from his kneeling position and turned to face the crowd.

"We have a chance, Tiberius gave us that chance, and in four months we have an opportunity to destroy the Blindspot."

As soon as Janus spoke of this, the Ministers moved to stop Janus. An attack cannot be planned without the approval of the ministry. But they were stopped by the Magus Knights. They looked towards the commanders of the first division but no one even batted an eye.

"In four months we can start to repay all the debt we owe to our fallen heroes. This monument in front of you isn't a representation of the deaths and sacrifices, but it's a testament of the promise we made to pay our debts. It was told to me that Sacrifices are necessary for the good of the many.Are you guys prepared to sacrifice for the debts we owe? I know I am, I will be standing with you in the front of the forces and will lead the battle, I will sacrifice myself for each one of you, will you? Too long we have been living under the darkness and fear, our hearts have become numb with fear, we have invited the darkness in our hearts and minds, will you fight a battle with me to get rid of darkness once and for all?"

As if on cue, thunder roared in the skies as the scores of people gathered shouted in unison. "We are with you."

Mathew roared over the shouts and cheers. "Wait everyone; we have a system here, Janus just because he is the leader of the Magus Knights cannot call for arms. The Ministry will decide a course of action, no one can act alone; we cannot fall to alawless system."

"Who risks their lives every day? Is it the Magus knights or the ministers who sit in their cozy chambers? Who stands by you? Who do you look up to? Who will lead you to deliverance? Today, we stand on a precipice, today we decide our future, either we follow the same path laid down by the ministry over the centuries, or we take control of our future and push forward and write our destinies by our own hands?"

The crowd cheered, "We will write our own future".

"Then let's put these traitors aside and stand by me towards a new dawn. Be it is the first division, the second division or the students of Academia Magoram, be it a citizen of the Central or a citizen of the Outer Sanctum, let's stand together and defeat this darkness. Too long have we let the politicians in the ministry get fat and ignore the plight of the common people, too long have we been comfortable within Central letting the Outer districts fight their own battle, no more."

The thunder roared above as the cowed roared on the field, and just like that the future course was decided.

Janus turned to Rayburn and put forward the sword left behind by Tiberius, "it's now yours, son, join your friends in the Academy and build a force like no other, hence forth you will be part of our Third Division".

As Rayburn feel to his knees and accepted the sword, he could see tears rolling down Janus' face. The rain hadn't yet started but for Rayburn those tears were nothing less than the impending thunderstorms.

Janus caught Rayburn's gaze, "We do not mourn our heroes, but seems the rain is crying on our behalf".

"Yes it's raining on our behalf" replied Rayburn.

Chapter 5

Threshold of the High Council

The atmosphere within the Academy was of excitement and hope the day after. The Students had gathered in the assemble hall to discuss the response to the call to arms by Janus and the magus Knights. They all felt the loss of Tiberius. Each had dreamt of a day when they will be join the ranks of the Magus Knights and ride out to slay the monsters that lay in wait outside the Sanctamonium. Each had dreamt of a day, when their dreams weren't filled with nightmares emanating from the Blindspot but rather of a bright day awaiting beyond the threshold.

Leandra Skylark, her golden hair a stark contrast to the wheatish skin, and Kael, the tall fair skinned well built upper classman, were the chosen leaders of the students. They were both popular and had a way with the students. Both were calm under strenuous situations and had often than not showed their skills both on and off the arena in which duels were held.

As Seraphim, Tomoe and Rayburn joined the group, for a moment, the eyes of Rayburn met with Leandra. Leandra felt a pang of guilt, as she remembered the comments she had passed on him the evening before, but his eyes seemed to be distant, a mirror to the storm brewing inside him. It was as if he didn't even see Leandra.

"We dreamt of this day when we will be join the Mages, and now we have the chance, lets gear up and show our support, let's stand by the Magus Knights", shouted one of the students. The others joined in the chorus, each looking towards Leandra and Kael for their support and leadership.

"Fighting the Darkseiths isn't like clearing an exam", boomed the voice of Seraphim; the severity of his voice silencing the entire group. This voice had the depth of the oceans, his heart filled with the grief of the loss of his parents and the loss of a dear brother. "We are still mages in training, many of us still struggle to conjure up effective magic and most of us do so using transmutation circles. Do you think the Darkseiths will give you time to draw circles in the middle of the battle? Rushing to our deaths isn't what the Janus had called us for. Our number won't matter if we simply become dead weight on the battlefield. Our jobs shouldn't be to slow the Magus Knights and become our protective shields; it should be to support them. First we should figure out our roles and plan a support system, rather than pick our swords and sticks to be fodder to the Darkseiths." A gloom fell over the assembly; they knew what Seraphim said though harsh was true. The Magus Knights were full-fledged mages with a lot of actual battle experience and still they faltered before the Darkseiths, what can a bunch of students achieve?

Tomoe could see the shift in the atmosphere and quickly interjected. "What my dear friend is trying to convey is that we should have a plan. We should use the time we have to train and be battle ready, we should talk to the teachers so that we can learn advance magic, we can also talk to the Magus Knights and the High Council for them to share information and take special classes so that we can prove our worth on the battlefield. There is always strength in numbers, and we are all mages, we are no less than the Knights, even if we cannot face off the higher Darkseiths alone, we are more than capable to take of the lesser ones. We just need a plan to act upon."

Leandra and Tomoe could see the light returning to the eyes of the students. Leandra gave an approving nod to Tomoe before taking over. "Let's divide our group into two for now. Kael and I will talk to the teachers and we can also hold trainings after the regular classes are over so that we can build up on what we know". Leandra and Kael were perfect for the job, no one objected to the decision. "Seraphim, Rayburn and Tomoe can act as a bridge between us and the Magus Knights and High Council, they already have ties both to Janus and Selene as we understand." Leandra passed a look towards Seraphim and Tomoe and they both nodded in unison. The other students also agreed to the arrangement.

The ancient doors of the High Council chamber groaned open as Seraphim Lumenhart led his companions through the threshold. Their boots resonated against the hallowed stone, a solemn drumbeat heralding their arrival. The grand hall stretched before them, its vaulted ceiling adorned with frescoes depicting the cosmos.

At the heart of this sanctum, seated at the head of an elongated table, was Selene Moonshadow. Mathew was removed from position and it was Selene who now served as the ambassador to the Academy and the Magus Knights.

"Welcome," Selene's voice cut through the silence, resonating with an authority that seemed to emanate from the chamber itself. "Your journey has led you to the heart of our conclave. Let us illuminate the path that lies shrouded before you." Her hand swept over the table as if beckoning forth the threads of destiny, inviting them to weave their fates into the tapestry of Sanctamonium's storied past. It was agreed that the students would be made aware of any information held by the council, so that they know what they were facing and to them their paths would be illuminated. Selene had requested the presence of the three to that effect.

Selene, poised at the head of the table, surveyed them with her inscrutable grey eyes. The air around her shimmered with subtle magic. "Your fervor speaks volumes of your commitment to the cause," she said, her tone even yet imbued with the gravity of eons. "The tale of Astolfo and Astaroth is woven into the very essence of this realm. It is a saga steeped in power, fraught with perils both seen and unseen."

She settled back into her chair, her hands resting calmly on the ancient wood of the council table. "I will share the history you crave, for it is your right as defenders of this city to wield its truths against the encroaching night." Her gaze softened slightly, an acknowledgment of their shared burden. "Prepare yourselves, for the path ahead is one of enlightenment and peril entwined."

"In times immemorial," she began, her gaze distant, "there stood two colossal figures upon the world stage: Astolfo, the Harbinger of Light, and Astaroth, the Shadow Weaver. Bound by fate and sundered by choice, their conflict transcended mere rivalry. It was a time when the divide between the masses grew to the highest pinnacle. The magic users though less in numbers controlled everything, the non magic users left to gather the leftovers. Though of the same race, they were considered beneath the mages. Astolfo was a soldier of the Second division, sold by his parents at young age into the academy. He quickly learnt the art of warfare and led Sanctamonium to victory against the neighboring countries without the support of the Mages. He rose through the ranks in a short time and became a commander at a young age. Being from the Outer Sanctums he was close to the people and helped every citizen. He ensured his forces visited the citizens to solve any concerns while on their daily rounds."

Rayburn couldn't help but imagine Tiberius; the similarity between the two was uncanny.

Selene continued, her hands unfolding like the pages of an ancient tome. "It was a time of kings and Sanctamonium had a royal family. Astaroth was one of the high ministers of the time, a born mage with unparallel mastery over the elements. He considered the others below him and was a talking walking symbol of pride. His origins are a bit hazy as the documents were lost during the Great War. Anyways he didn't take lightly to Astolfo when they met and wasn't too keen about his popularity. Later Astolfo was chosen to be part of the ministers in the king's council."

"After a few years, while studying the scripts and books on magic, Astolfo discovered a secret to bring magic to the masses."

"Transmutation Circles", Tomoe interjected.

"Precisely", said Selene and continued. "This created further rifts between the two and one day Astaroth through a Royal Decree banned the use of Transmutation circles. He wanted to control magic and its users and have everything for himself. This caused a civil war, Astolfo and the masses on one side and Astaroth and the mages on the other with some defectors here and there.It was a war that raged across realms, a cataclysmic battle that threatened to rend the fabric of the cosmos. Finally a truce was brokered between the factions and they met at the grand council hall, now called by a separate name."

"The Eclipse", said Rayburn, his eyes focused on the ground.

"Precisely" said Selene. "But there something fell apart. Rose, the love of Astaroth was killed, again the details are not clear, but it led to a confrontation between the two. From the heart of chaos," Selene intoned, "they conjured spells of unimaginable potency. Astaroth murdered the Royal family who had brokered the meeting and in his rage he wanted to destroy everything. He would have but somewhere between the chaoses their magic birthed an anomaly—a Blindspot where reality wavers and dreams hold sway. Astaroth vanished or was destroyed and killed, depending on the interpretation and the world was divided. We do not know what happened to the other kingdoms, nor do we know of what happened afterwards to the Royal bloodline."

"Anyways then the monuments you see everywhere were created by Astolfo as a reminder of the time when the world was almost destroyed and what the misuse of magic could bring forth. He spent the remainder of his life teaching the use transmutation circles to the people and over time it became the norm for magic users.The knowledge of how magic was used before that is lost and most books and scripts were destroyed during the war." She paused to let the information settle in, it was a long history spread over decades, made concise for their benefit. Some of the aspects were kept hidden due to various reasons decided by the ministry. The story was known to every kid in the Sanctamonium, it was story the trio had grown up with but still a lot was left unsaid. Seraphim couldn't help but wonder about Rose and Astaroth, he was always the villain, imagining love in him except for power was a difficult thought. Tomoe wondered why Astolfo didn't write the history for the people to know, the story they heard was built in bits and pieces. The story of the two was still an enigma.

"Keep in mind that these are deciphered from ancient texts and many of the things are open to interpretations, but this is the common consensus of what happened a thousand years ago. What we know is that the Obscuratus

Umbra is not merely a void but a chasm fed by the dreams of those who dare to imagine."

"Every dream," Selene continued, her silver hair glinting in the half-light, "ripples through the cosmos, plucked from slumber by the Blindspot's insatiable hunger. It is a storm of unfulfilled desires and feared nightmares; a force that grows stronger with each wayward dreamer's energy it ensnares."

The chamber resonated with the gravity of Selene's next words, a solemn hush falling over the trio as they leaned in. "To comprehend our plight," she began, her voice ringing with an otherworldly timbre, "One must first understand the forces that threaten Sanctamonium."

"Darkseiths," Seraphim said, clenching his teeth. "Creatures born from the Blindspot's shadow, correct?"

"Indeed," Selene confirmed. "They are the antithesis of all we hold dear—harbingers of anarchy, born from the chaos at the edges of our dreams. They seek to unravel the fabric of reality, to return us to the void from whence the cosmos sprang."

Tomoe shifted, her brow creased with concern, "and the Blindspot itself? Is it sentient or merely a breeding ground for these abominations?"

"It is both, and yet neither," Selene replied cryptically. "A nexus of unformed potential, a wellspring of nightmare given form by the fears of dreamers. It grows more potent with each passing day, fed by the subconscious dread of our citizens. We do know that it has the power to revive the fallen Darkseiths, so even if every Darkseith is destroyed which is present today, till the Blindspot stands there can be no victory."

"Then our mission," Rayburn interjected, his stoic facade betraying a flicker of emotion, "is to sever this connection? To starve the Blindspot of its nourishment?"

"Not entirely, fear and nightmares cannot be starved but can be controlled, its effects limited. The Blindspot feeds not only on the energies of the dream realm, but also on the fear it sows in the hearts of our people."

She could see that the expressions on the trio becoming grim as they were beginning to absorb the gravity of the task that lay ahead.

"Remember, the magic of dreams transcends all barriers," Selene continued, her tone infused with the wisdom of the ages. "It connects us to the multiverse, to the infinite possibilities that lie beyond the veil of reality. Harness this connection, and the Blindspot shall become nothing more than a fading shadow."

Their hearts buoyed by Selene's guidance, the trio exchanged glances, each seeing the reflection of their determination in the other's eyes. They were ready to confront the unknown, to face the ever-encroaching gloom with the light of their combined wills.

"Trust in yourselves, in the bonds that unite you, and in the destiny that awaits you," Selene intoned, her final words echoing like a prophecy set into the stones of time.

With renewed purpose etched upon their features, Seraphim, Rayburn, and Tomoe turned towards the grand archway of the High Council chamber. Their footsteps reverberated across the ancient stones, each step a defiant march against the encroaching darkness.

Back at the Academy they discussed what they learnt with Leandra and Kael. Kael decided to keep the information to them for now without informing the other students. "Deciding the flow of information is also a job of the leader", smiled Kael looking towards Seraphim. He put his large hand on Seraphim's shoulder, "I know you meant well in the assembly, you were concerned about the students, it's a quality every leader should have, but words have a lot of influence. It can build armies or it can make a kingdom fall. You have much to learn, but you are on the right path."

Seraphim had seem the effect his words had on the students, he didn't consider himself as their leader, he was just a student same as them. He didn't plan to lead anyone; he was always content doing what his heart desired. But it seemed it was a job that has been thrust upon him now, not just him but Rayburn and Tomoe as well. He felt grateful that Tomoe was by his side, it was she who was better suited for the job anyways. Rayburn's presence was enough to sway crowds and without words he could influence more than Seraphim ever could. He was starting to understand the position he was in and how every action mattered, he couldn't but marvel at the age old heroes and the hero in front of him, Janus. He was coming to grasp the reality of the burden when other people put their hopes on him.

Chapter 6

Moonlit Magic Chamber

Selene Moonshadow ushered Seraphim, Rayburn, and Tomoe through the towering archway of the Academy of Magus. The training they started under her hadn't come to an end yet, with final few chapters of her tutelage still to be taught. The threshold gave way to a vast chamber where the thrum of latent power resonated against ancient stone walls. Ethereal light cascaded from high windows, casting an otherworldly glow upon rows of dusty tomes and arcane instruments that lined the room. As they entered, a tangible current of energy brushed their skin, the very air alive with the whispers of a thousand spells waiting to be born.

"Here," Selene's voice cut through the charged silence, "we shall begin the final phase of our training."

"Stand together," Selene instructed, her grey robe reflecting the gravity of her words. "Clasp hands. Unity is the bedrock upon which your strength will be built."

Tomoe Shinsei, with her elegant poise and thoughtful eyes, extended her hands first. Seraphim followed, his fingers interlocking with hers, their touch a silent vow of shared purpose. Rayburn completed the circle, his hand finding Seraphim's.

"Feel it," Selene continued, "The pulse of the multiverse beats within each of you. Synchronization is not merely about timing—it is the harmony of souls, the confluence of dreams that forges unparalleled might."

The trio closed their eyes, breaths falling into a unified rhythm. The magic swelled around them—an ominous yet awe-inspiring tide of potential that danced at the edges of comprehension. They could feel their heartbeats aligning with the ring of the bell tower, ever audible from any corner of the Sanctamonium. The rhythmic pulse filled them, encroaching on their souls.

"Patience," Selene intoned, sensing their frustration. "Magic is both art and science, a delicate balance between force and finesse. See beyond the physical; reach into the fabric of the cosmos itself."

Under Selene's patient tutelage, the trio's determination kindled anew. Seraphim relaxed his rigid posture, and with a deep inhalation, he surrendered to the currents of the unseen winds. A gust swirled around his fingertips with newfound resolve.

Rayburn centered himself, envisioning the tranquil depths of an ancient lake, untouched by the turmoil of the surface world. A droplet formed, suspended midair before him—a perfect orb

Tomoe's inner strength ignited, her will, a beacon calling to the fire that slumbered within the dreamscape. With a gentle exhalation, a warm glow emanated from her hand, a delicate fire that danced in harmony with her steady heartbeat.

"Control is paramount," Selene reminded them, her gaze unyielding. "But now, let us weave these threads together. Unity in diversity shall create a tapestry more formidable than any single strand alone."

The trio exchanged determined glances, nodding to each other before turning their focus inward once again. Seraphim's breeze began to encircle the group, a gentle zephyr that carried the promise of storms. Rayburn's water orb expanded, mist rising to meet the wind, while Tomoe's fire sent tendrils of warmth spiraling upward, licking at the cool droplets.

"Harmonize your energies," Selene coaxed. "Let wind guide, water shape, and fire energize. Together!"

The elements danced a ballet of creation and destruction, merging into a spectacular maelstrom above their heads. The air sizzled where fire met mist, steam rising to fuel Seraphim's winds while Rayburn's water cooled the flames, preventing them from scorching the air they sought to command.

The vortex waned as the trio gradually withdrew their magic, sweat glistening their foreheads—a physical tribute to the metaphysical ordeal. They stood panting, surrounded by the dissipating remnants of their collaboration, each face alight with the glow of accomplishment and the dawning realization of their burgeoning prowess.

Tomoe, her eyes as grateful as her tone spoke, "Your lessons forge us anew. We promise to honor your teachings with a relentless pursuit of mastery." Seraphim and Rayburn nodded in agreement.

Selene received their thanks with a nod, her piercing grey eyes reflecting pride and expectation. "Your journey ahead is fraught with shadows that hunger for the unwary," she cautioned, her tone imbued with the gravity of her station. "Let the light of your determination dispel the darkness."

In the quiet aftermath, as his companions departed to seek much-needed rest, Seraphim lingered. His gaze turned inward, and he marveled at the transformation wrought within him; where once uncertainty gnawed at his spirit, confidence now flourished. The winds he could summon danced to his command, no longer capricious gales but an extension of his will.

Chapter 7

The Unfinished Mission

It had been almost a month since the call to arms had been declared by Janus. The students in the Academy were busy with the classes, the teachers had started teaching advance magic aimed at warfare tactics, and there were frequent meetings with the high council representatives and the Magus Knights. After regular classes Leandra and Kael led the students through duels to teach them about actual warfare so that the students could gain experience of actual combat. The trainings were also fruitful in determining the classes of the students and dividing them into warlocks, high mages and healers, each having a specific task in the battle ahead. The warlocks would become the attacking force, the Mages being the support and healers taking care of the injured.

Tomoe had started training with her dual blades, a warlock in her every fiber. She was among the best fighters, with even the seniors having a difficult time with her in the duals. Seraphim and Rayburn had the affinity for both the classes; they could act as a mage, given their mastery over the elements as well as a warlock given their combat skills. Kael was a warlock at heart and Leandra was difficult to be put in a definite box.

News had arrived that Satori was to address the students today. It was rare for the second in command to grace the students with his presence, so there was an air of excitement in the Academy. The students settled in the assembly with Satori taking the chair on the stage.

"We have a mission in hand, and it was decided by the Magus Knights to test your mettle to see how you will fair in the upcoming battle". His words were crisp and direct; he didn't have time to spend on the students and definitely didn't care much about them. It was apparent from his demeanor that it was a waste of time for him. "Obviously one of the Magus Knights will lead the mission and you are to act as the support. As you all know Tiberius along with his comrades had ventured into the Eclipse and was able to bring back vital information. Since then the activity within the eclipse had been diminished. We assume that he must have faced a higher Darkseith, a Sin or a Vicar maybe, and were able to gravely injure it. The lesser Darkseiths are controlled by the higher ones and they have a strict hierarchy. Anyways we plan to venture into the Eclipse again to gather more information. Anything that tips the scale to our side even a little is of paramount importance now. So we need volunteers from your side, three to be exact for the expedition." He sat down as soon as he completed saying his piece.

Leandra, Kael, Seraphim and Tomoe looked at each speaking with their eyes, they needed a quick consultation. Rayburn on the other hand stood up, touched the hilt of the Gleaming Sorrow, and without even looking up, started walking towards Satori, signifying him volunteering for the mission.

"I believe I should' volunteer and go for the mission", said Seraphim.

"I should join you", said Tomoe, "we can test what we learned from Selene. Anyways we work together better and can support Rayburn, I don't think he is going to back down in anycase. He owes it to Tiberius".

"I concur", agreed Leandra and Kael, "and we can continue with the trainings here, we have been making good progress."

Seraphim Lumenhart's silhouette cut a sharp figure against the twilight that caressed the edge of the Blindspot. He scanned the abyss before him, and his slender fingers curled into fists at his side. Beside him, Rayburn Wilder and Tomoe Shinsei stood as a testament to their shared valor, their postures taut with anticipation. The air was thick with the weight of unspoken oaths and the silent camaraderie of warriors bound by a cause greater than them. It was the first time they were to venture into the darkness they had resolved to conquer and the anticipation was making their heart skip its beats.

They were lead by Satori himself, an outcome none expected, maybe to protect Rayburn, the death of Tiberius weighed heavily on him as well. "Stay beside me, we donot need heroes in this journey, but members of a team who can work together and watch each other's back. I have made a promise to bring all three of you back in one piece; do not fail me in doing so."

As their boots whispered across the boundary, darkness enveloped them like a shroud spun from the very fabric of night. The Blindspot swallowed their forms, its breath an oppressive force that robbed the warmth from their flesh and cast long shadows upon their spirits. The air grew dense as if charged with unseen currents of malevolent power, its pressure mounting against their chests with each advancing step.

The Blindspot responded not with sound but with a creeping chill that sought to claim them, to seep into marrow and memory alike. It tested their mettle, probed for weaknesses within their ranks, yet found only the unwavering tenacity of those who walked the path of heroes.

Together, they delved into an extension of the Blindspot, called the "Eclipse". It was once a great hall where the representatives of the different kingdoms met, to discuss their affairs and to settle disputes. Satori led the way, his well built frame cutting through the suffocating gloom of the Eclipse like a blade. His piercing brown eyes scanned the jagged landscape with unwavering vigilance. The air around them hung stagnant as if time was reluctant to proceed in this forsaken place. Each step they took was silent, absorbed by the omnipresent darkness that enveloped the group like a shroud. Their path lit only by the faint glow emanating from Tomoe's fingertips, twisted and turned through the unnatural terrain—a mirror to the chaos that lay ahead. Rayburn walked close behind.

"Curiosity or caution?" Satori asked after a while, his soft voice slicing through the silence. They had ventured quite inside the eclipse. It was less of a question and more of a challenge thrown towards the new adventurers.

Seraphim, ever the leader, stepped closer to the anomaly, his gaze locked upon its mesmerizing depths. "We press on," he declared, his voice a quiet force against the darkness. "Our quest lies beyond fear."

The group exchanged glances, each pair of eyes reflecting the same resolute fire. In unison, they ventured ahead, hearts pounding with a mix of trepidation and anticipation. As they drew nearer, the shadows within the eclipse seemed to pulse as if beckoning them to enter its embrace.

With a hiss that shattered the quiet, a creature lunged from the shadows, its form a grotesque tapestry of nightmares. Multiple eyes glinted like wet obsidian, and limbs bent at impossible angles, skittering across the cracked earth with eerie grace. Each member of the party tensed, ready for combat, yet these beings did not attack; instead, they circled at a distance, a silent threat weaving through the dark.

"Stay vigilant," Satori whispered; his voice steady. "They are testing us."

"Janus would not have faltered here," Rayburn said, more to himself than to the others.

An archway loomed ahead, gnarled by time and dark arts, beckoning them onward. With measured steps, they entered the hidden chamber, its walls covered in veils. Here lay the remnants of knowledge long forsaken, rows of ancient tomes bound in leather that whispered secrets, artifacts that thrummed with latent power.

"Look for anything that may unveil the Blind spot's lineage," Satori instructed, his celestial-patterned robes grazing the dusty floor as he approached a weathered shelf.

Something caught Rayburn's attention, a reflection from the light emanating from Tomoe's orb. He went near the origin. "Here," Rayburn called out, holding aloft a medallion. "This bears the mark of Astolfo, the lore speaks of his clash with Astaroth."

"This place can hold knowledge critical to our cause", Satori exclaimed, "Every little fragment can shine a light to the darkened path."

The chamber's deceptive stillness shattered as a misplaced step upon an ancient rune sent tremors through the stone floor. Walls, lined with secrets of ages past, groaned ominously initiating their inward march. Seraphim's heart thudded against his ribs, a drumbeat in sync with the encroaching slabs of rock. The air, already thick with magic and must, grew denser, squeezing breaths from their lungs as the space narrowed.

The darkness in the chamber wasn't helping in the escape."Tomoe, bring forth your sphere of fire", instructed Seraphim. As Tomoe made the orb of light into a ball of fire, Seraphim reacted and using his wind magic worked in tandem with Tomoe. He pushed the orb higher into the ceiling and gushes of air emanating from Seraphim spread the fire across the ceiling of the chamber, illuminating the entire space. He created a wall using his magic so that the fire remained constricted high on the ceiling. Rayburn jumped into action as well; using his water magic he created another wall just below the fire. The water reflected and refracted the light to create a dance of colors within the chamber, yet ensuring that the air below doesn't heat up, keeping the temperature in control. Satori was impressed by the quick thinking and the cohesive effort of the group, even skilled mages have a hard time working together, but it was not the time to marvel at the trio. Time was against them as the walls kept inching forward, determined to crush them within.

And then, as if conjured by his will, a glimmer caught his eye—a sliver of hope in the form of an inconspicuous lever nestled within the chamber's elaborate carvings, nearly indistinguishable from the ornate designs surrounding it.

Without hesitation, he dashed towards the wall, his comrades bolstering their defenses behind him. Satori's hand wrapped around the cold metal, and with a grunt of exertion fueled by necessity and the raw instinct to survive, he pulled.

A resounding click echoed through the chamber like the tolling of a bell, and the walls ceased their advance with mere moments to spare. A collective exhale filled the space, and the group slumped against the once-threatening barricades, relief flooding their senses.

"By the cosmos..." Rayburn breathed, disbelief etched into his features as he looked at Satori. "You've done it."

"Only together," Satori replied, meeting the gazes of his allies. "Let us press on. The Eclipse awaits our challenge, and we shall not be found wanting."

The corridor widened, revealing an expansive chamber where the oppressive gloom retreated marginally before the presence of something ancient and powerful. Dominating the far wall was an immense mural, its surface alive with ethereal luminescence that danced across the depicted chaos.

"Behold," Tomoe whispered, her voice barely above the hush of shadows, "the battle between Astolfo Starlight and Astaroth Darkstorm."

The image was of a battle between light and dark, celestial brilliance clashing against abyssal torrents. There stood Astolfo, his hair a cascade of shimmering stardust, locked in combat with Astaroth, whose figure was a well of shadow that threatened to engulf all.

"Look at the fury in their eyes," Rayburn murmured, his gaze tracing the arc of Astolfo's dream-forged blade as it met the dark steel of Astaroth's scepter.

They lingered no longer than necessary, the gravity of history heavy upon them. The lingering questions from the meeting with Selene still fresh in their minds. The path called them forth, spiraling downward into the bowels of the Eclipse. The air grew colder, the silence more profound, as if the very void itself held its breath.

At last, they stumbled upon a shrine forgotten by time, its stone altar adorned with runes that flickered faintly like dying stars. The surrounding walls were etched with the same script, one that spoke of the fabric of dreams and the cosmos.

"Can you make sense of this?" Tomoe asked, her fingers tracing the glowing lines with reverence.

"The prophecy," Satori began, his voice steady despite the awe that gripped him; "It speaks of balance. When day and night converge within the heart of darkness, the Blindspot shall unravel."

"Is it talking about an eclipse?" Tomoe remarked "isn't it a bit much. A part of Blindspot called The Eclipse, talking about an eclipse as a suitable time to conquer the Blindspot?"

The sarcasm of the meaning did feel strange to all, but they didn't have much time to contemplate the situation.

The silent expanse of the Blindspot trembled as a chill wind howled through its void, and Seraphim Lumenhart's breath caught in his throat. The air thickened with malice, and from the darkness coalesced a figure of sheer terror— a Vicar wrought from nightmares, its silhouette a smudge against the oppressive gloom.

"Stand ready," Satori commanded, his voice cutting through the stifling air as he raised his hand, light magic gathering at his fingertips like the first rays piercing through dawn.

Tomoe brandished her twin blades, their edges gleaming with a preternatural sharpness, as she stood shoulder-to-shoulder with her companions.

The Vikar, a higher level Darkseith advanced. It had a human like form, with its head missing above its nostrils. It was as if a hammer had fallen on its head flattening the surface. Without its eyes and a head to think, it was a sight of sheer terror. Its form undulating with darkness, tendrils reaching out like claws seeking to snuff out the light they carried within them.A cacophony of whispers filled the air, an ancient language of despair that sought to fracture their resolve.

Seraphim struck first, arcs of wind slicing through shadow, while Rayburn drowned the very earth beneath the feet summoning water. Tomoe danced between the dark tendrils, her blades a blur of precision and grace, each strike bringing forth a volley of fire.

"Focus! Together!" Seraphim called out, his blue eyes afire with purpose. They moved as one, a unit bound by trust forged in the crucible of shared trials.

Satori unleashed a torrent of elemental fury, fire and thunder amalgamating into a storm directed at the heart of the guardian. But each assault only seemed to feed the creature, its essence growing denser, more potent.

"Unyielding," Rayburn growled, as he channeled his magic into a protective dome, shielding them from a crushing blow that shook the very foundation of the Blindspot.

"Remember our training," Tomoe reminded them, her voice a bastion of calm amidst chaos.

In a moment of clarity, Seraphim understood. It wasn't merely about striking down the Vicar; it was a test of harmony, of balance.The group's combined might coalesced around Seraphim, who focused it into a singular point of brilliance. As the light met the shadow, a resounding boom echoed, and for an instant, day and night co-existed in union.

With a shudder that rippled through reality, the guardian let out a soundless scream and dissipated into a cloud of dust that sparkled with residual magic before fading entirely.

This was the opening they were waiting for. They retreated without a word among themselves, running through the path they had taken to reach the entrance of the eclipse. The somber sky of Sanctamonium loomed over them, a tapestry of twilight hues that seemed to hold its breath as Seraphim Lumenhart and his allies stepped out from the gaping maw of the Blindspot. The air was crisp with the scent of impending rain, a stark contrast to the suffocating darkness they had left behind. Their silhouettes were etched against the dying light, each figure resolute—carrying the weight of prophecy and a future unwritten.

"The Vicar was indeed weakened, your brother was a true champion among champions" Satori said, as he put his hand on Rayburn. The marks on it were definitely from the Gleaming sorrow, marks we have seen many times before. I guess it's fast retreat was also due to the fear the gleaming sorrow etched in its memory."

"Darkseiths feel fear too?" inquired Tomoe, "Still breathless from the narrow escape".

"Every living thing has feared within, it's the essence of being alive" replied Satori.

Now safe outside the shadows of the Blindspot, they took a sigh of relief. The change in tone and demeanor Satori had was a testament of his acknowledgement of the trio. They decided to camp in the outer sanctum for the night, before returning to the Central to inform of their progress. Satori wanted the trio to take rest for the night, it was the first time that an entire group made it back alive from eclipse, thought some of the credit goes to the sacrifice made by Tiberius and his team, the feat attained by these mere students wasn't something to be brushed off.

Chapter 7

Pandemonium in the Outer Districts

The next morning was a testament to the despair that the darkness brought forth, what seemed like a victory last night, rang with the bells of impending doom.

The air was thick with the acrid scent of smoke as Seraphim Lumenhart, Rayburn Wilder, and Tomoe Shinsei navigated the pandemonium that had seized the Outer Districts. The once-vibrant market streets, alive with the jingle of Shades and the laughter of children chasing through stalls, now echoed with the cacophony of terror: screams punctuated by the crash of buildings succumbing to shadow and flame.

"Rayburn, to your left!" Seraphim called out, his voice barely slicing through the din as a hulking Darkseith lunged from the swirling darkness. The monstrous beings had descended without warning, their arrival heralding chaos as they tore through the district's defenses like a scourge.

The warlock's formal attire, once pristine and symbolizing his valor, was marred with soot and the evidence of battle. His resolve, however, remained unblemished.

Beside him, Tomoe moved with lethal grace, her petite frame a deceptive mask for the warrior within. The marketplace had become an arena where her swift strikes were her discourse, her blade singing a silent requiem for the fallen. She fought not just for herself or for Rayburn, to whom her loyalty was bound by shared scars, but for every soul whose dream was to live free from fear.

Seraphim, his slender form cutting through the smog, channeled the elemental forces at his command. The juxtaposition of destruction against the backdrop of the Outer Districts—a place teeming with life and labor—only fueled his determination. It was here, amid the hum of artisans and farmers that the heart of Sanctamonium beat strongest and he would not let it be stilled.

"Keep pushing them back!" he shouted, casting a glance at the sky where smoke battled the twilight, each vying to paint the canvas of their world.

Above them, the banners that once swayed gently in the breeze now hung tattered, the sigils of Sanctamonium's military divisions scorched and indiscernible. The soldiers and knights, both magical and non-magical, rushed to form barricades, their ranks a testament to the city's resilience.

Through the haze of destruction, the trio glimpsed the citizens of the Outer Districts, their faces etched with fear as they fled from the encroaching shadows. Amongst them were those who dared hope, their gazes fixed upon the mages and defenders battling the darkness. They saw not only the clash of power but also the courage that defied despair.

As Seraphim, Rayburn, and Tomoe stood together, surrounded by the ruins of what had been a bastion of commerce and community, the stark contrast between the thriving life of the Outer Districts and the suffocating grip of the Darkseith invasion became a rallying cry. This was more than a battle; it was a declaration that the light of Sanctamoniumwould not be extinguished, not while its protectors still drew breath. The Magus Knights had joined in the battle as well.

Janus's fingers danced through the air, tracing ethereal symbols that ignited with a spectral glow. The elemental forces at his command responded with fervor, weaving a protective gale around him that deflected the oncoming assault of the Darkseiths. He focused, eyes blazing with an azure intensity that mirrored the tempest he conjured, hurling bolts of lightning at the shadowy figures that surged forward.

Beside him, his second-in-command channeled his anguish into power. His weapons—an amalgam of warlock craft and sheer will—hummed with enchantments, each strike against the monstrous foes imbued with eldritch might. The air crackled around him, hissing as his blade cut through the darkness, severing limbs with precision.

The Darkseiths were a grotesque tapestry of nightmares woven into reality, their forms a cloud of terror that chilled the soul. Their claws, like scythes, glistened with a sinister sheen, eager to rend and tear. The glowing red orbs that served as their eyes pierced through the smoke and chaos. Around them swirled an aura of darkness so profound that it seemed to swallow light, an eerie umbra that hungered for despair.

As the three companions fought in unison, their resolve unbroken by the horrors that faced them, the Outer Districts echoed with the clash of magic and malice. With each passing moment, the tide of battle shifted; a testament to the tenacity of those who would stand against the shadows.

Seraphim's breath came in measured bursts, the air crackling around him as he summoned the raw elements to his command. With a sweep of his hand, a gust of wind hurtled towards a pack of Darkseiths that had cornered a group of fleeing citizens. The wind, charged with electric fury, flung the monsters back, their cries piercing the tumultuous night.

"Stay close!" Seraphim shouted over the din of battle, his blue eyes, fierce and resolute, scanned the chaos for his companions.

Rayburn, brandished his enchanted weapon with lethal precision. A warlock's chant escaped his lips, the stream of water brought forth cut through the Darkseith onslaught like blades and knives through butter.

Tomoe, her silhouette a striking contrast against the flames that consumed the Outer Districts, moved with purposeful fluidity. Her twin blades, an extension of her will, danced through the air, leaving arcs of silver in their wake.

Each strike was a promise, a silent vow to uphold the sanctity of their beloved home.

The Darkseiths regrouped, their numbers seemingly endless, a tide of malevolence surging forward. Yet, for each that fell, another rose to take its place, their red eyes alight with savage hunger.

In the face of overwhelming odds, Seraphim's control over the elements never waned, a tempest of wind at his beck and call. Rayburn's incantations resonated with ancient power, his weapons cleaving through shadowy flesh with supernatural force. Tomoe, ever the eye of the storm, found the seams in the enemy's onslaught, her blades whispering death to any who dared breach their defenses.

Their hearts thrummed with adrenaline, each beat a drum of war that drove them forward. There was no room for doubt, no moment for fear—only the unshakeable certainty that they would stand and fight, that the lives of innocents and the future of Sanctamonium hinged upon their courage.

As Darkseith after Darkseith fell before them, the trio's synergy was unmistakable, their determination manifesting in a display of arcane mastery and martial prowess. And in this dire hour, their will remained unbroken; their spirits alight with the undying flame of resistance.

"Rayburn!" The name escaped Seraphim's lips, a desperate plea as he watched his comrade stagger beneath the weight of a monstrous Darkseith. The creature's claws were like curved daggers, each one gleaming with a promise of death. It pinned Rayburn to the cracked cobblestones, its glowing red eyes a pair of malevolent stars in the smog-filled sky.

Fear clutched at Seraphim's heart, a fear not for himself, but for the brother-in-arms struggling beneath the hulking shadow. Tomoe's silhouette darted past, her twin blades a blur of silver, seeking to sever the creature's intent from its limbs.

The air trembled with the power of their struggle, the determination of the trio resonating as a silent vow to stand against this tide of darkness.

Around them, Sanctamonium wept in ruins. Buildings, once proud and tall, lay fractured, their innards spilled onto the streets. A tapestry shop, its vibrant colors now dulled by soot, crumbled as another wave of dark creatures surged forth, reducing it to rubble. Innocents, their faces etched with terror, fled in all directions, clutching whatever fragments of their lives they could salvage. Children cried out for lost parents, their wails a haunting counterpoint to the symphony of chaos.

"Focus on the living. Drive them back!"

Janus and Satori left the Knights behind and jumped into the Blindspot. Their aim was to find the leader, maybe the Vicar Satori had faced earlier or a Sin hiding just beyond in the darkness. The remaining Knights fought tooth and nail against the co ordinate onslaught, but the numbers were too great.

Tomoe, her senses heightened by the peril, read the battlefield as if it were a grim tapestry. Observing a cluster of Darkseiths attempting to flank them, she whistled sharply—a signal understood without words. With a swift motion, she unleashed a series of strikes imbued with the uncommon attribute of cut, slicing through the eerie darkness that clung to their foes.

It was then, that reinforcements arrived—mages and defenders of Sanctamonium, each marked by the resolve that shone in their eyes even as shadows loomed over the district. Leandra Skylark, joined the fray with a flourish of her hand, summoning torrents of light that bathed the area in a protective glow. Other mages channeled their connection to the cosmos, weaving spells of Wind and Thunder that roared through the ranks of the Darkseiths.

"Stand firm! Together, we are unassailable!" Tenex, one of the Magus Knights rallied, bolstered by the sight of allies converging on their location. The camaraderie among the Knights was palpable, transcending spoken language as they moved in concert, their combined might a testament to the bonds forged in the heat of countless battles.

Each new arrival lent their strength to the cause, their magic blending seamlessly. Soldiers from the First Division, though bereft of magical prowess, stood shoulder to shoulder with the Magus Knights, their weapons raised in defiance of the dark tide that threatened to consume all they held dear.

Amidst the whirling melee, Seraphim caught Tomoe's eye, a silent acknowledgement exchanged between them.

Their united front against the Darkseiths was no longer just a desperate stand; it was a declaration—a promise that the light within them would never yield to the consuming void.

Flames licked the sky, casting an infernal glow upon the battlefield as Tomoe, summoned a gale that swept through the ranks of retreating Darkseiths. With each gust, their shadows waned, the eerie darkness that clung to them like a shroud beginning to dissipate under the relentless onslaught of wind and flame.

"Push forward!" Rayburn Wilder's voice, laden with authority, thundered. Swords alive with slices of streams, cleaved through the horde cutting down the monstrous entities as their red eyes dimmed, their shrill cries dwindling into silence.

The tide had turned; the once-overwhelming mass of Darkseiths now thinned by the combined efforts of Sanctamonium's defenders. Every spell cast, every blade swung, carried the weight of the Outer Districts' determination to survive. The air, once thick with the stench of terror, now pulsed with the energy of impending victory.

As the last of the creatures fell, the Outer Districts exhaled a collective breath held too long in suspense. Buildings stood crumbling, testament to the ferocity of the attack, but they still stood—a symbol of the resilience of the people who called these vibrant streets home. Smoldering ruins sent plumes of smoke skyward, but beneath it all, there was life—beaten, yet unbroken.

Seraphim, Rayburn, and Tomoe gathered amidst the debris, their breaths coming in heavy gasps. They shared a look of mutual acknowledgment, their bond forged stronger in the crucible of conflict. They had defended their home, not just with their magic, but with their very souls.

As night descended upon the weary warriors, they allowed themselves a moment of respite, a brief interlude of peace in a world where darkness loomed ever close. They had earned it, and they stood ready for whatever would come next, united and unyielding.

Janus surveyed the damage with a furrowed brow, his mind racing with the implications of the attack. The air, thick with the scent of char and magic, spoke of a war far from concluded. The ground was wet with blood, the soft soil had turned murky. Though they emerged victorious there was a heavy toll that had been paid. He knelt down beside the lifeless body of a boy, a teen at best. He was wearing the colors of the academy of mages. He would have rushed out to help his comrades, his friends in this battle. Where his eyes should have shone with the promise of a future, now they lay blank and grey. He steeled himself against the scene before him, "we do not mourn our heroes", he said to himself as he closed the eyes of the young boy. "Except for his parents,he will be just another name carved into the monument of heroes; no one will remember his sacrifice and heroism. I promise you I will remember you and each one who has fallen today". He knew the Darkseiths would return, perhaps in greater numbers, drawn by the very essence Sanctamonium had fought so valiantly to protect. "Whatever respite we have now, it is but a fleeting shadow," Janus murmured. The weight of leadership pressed upon him, as heavy as the debris that littered the streets.

Rayburn Wilder stood beside him, "we've pushed back the darkness today," he said, his voice a low rumble, "but it's a darkness that learns, adapts. You have taught me that much."

"We must prepare, ready ourselves, for what is the cost of sacrifice against the cost of human lives," Janus whispered before relieving himself to his quarters.

Chapter 8

The Shrouded Chamber

The heavy door creaked open, and Rayburn stepped into the shrouded chamber deep within the bowels his house, into a chamber he himself was unaware existed. His pulse throbbed in his ears, a rhythmic testament to the heady blend of anticipation and anxiety that coursed through him. Around him, the room was enshrouded in shadows, save for an orb of light hovering above a table laden with mysteriousgear. The air held a scent of ancient parchment and smoldering incense, hinting at the arcane rituals performed here.

He found himself amidst a few chosen initiates, their faces etched with solemnity as they gathered in silent accord. Each one bore the mark of Janus Gravestone's tutelage—their eyes, like Rayburn's, reflecting a tempestuous dance of hope and reverence for the master they sought to emulate. They were the chosen acolytes, united by a secret bond formed under the tutelage of a man whose very name invoked awe.

His gaze swept over the clandestine assembly, his dark eyes harboring an unspoken yearning—validation from the very man who had rescued him from obscurity and shaped his destiny with the gentle hands of a sculptor. Unbeknownst to his companions, it was not just another lesson that brought him to this sanctum; it was the promise of transcending his limitations, of touching the very essence of the magical cosmos that beckoned to him through his dreams.

The anticipation thickened around him like a tangible cloak, every breath he drew laced with the gravity of what was to unfold. He had trained, fought, and bled to earn his place in this inner circle, and now, as he moved closer to the heart of the chamber, he could feel the weight of the unseen forces that swirled around the room—forces that pulsed with the potential to either exalt or extinguish.

"Rayburn," Janus' voice cut through the silence, resonant and laced with power. It was a call to step forward, a summons to embrace the unknown.

He advanced, his heart a relentless drum, each step heavy with the burden of trust he placed in the man who had become his mentor, his father in all but blood. Rayburn approached the center of the circle, where the light from the orb cast an otherworldly glow.

"Remove your garment and recline upon the table," he commanded, pointing a scarred finger that had directed countless incantations and spells.

Rayburn shed his shirt, the fabric slipping from his shoulders to reveal a well builttorso,a testimony to his endless training and strict regimen. His skin prickled against the chill of the room.

Lying back on the cold surface, Rayburn's heart thrummed a cadence of loyalty and fear. He steeled himself, the icy touch of the metal seeping into his bones.

Janus leaned over him, eyes reflecting a zeal that bordered on the divine. "This experiment," he began, voice laced with the gravity of eons, "is designed to magnify your innate capacities. To tap into the dreamtide's ebb and flow, harnessing it's might to augment your magic beyond the ordinary bounds."

"Imagine, Rayburn," Janus continued, his tone imbuing each word with portentous weight, "the latent potential within you, unleashed and refined. You shall wield powers rivaled by few, a paragon among Warlocks and Mages alike."

"Your dedication has brought you to this precipice," Janus intoned, a sculptor poised to mold his finest creation. "Now, we embark upon a journey where heroes are forged bringing forth what lay within."

Janus' hands, steady as the ancient obelisks that guarded the Magus Academy's forbidden vaults, hovered momentarily above a weathered leather roll. With a deliberate motion, he unfurled it upon a side table, revealing an array of sharp tools glinting ominously under the dim light—a harbinger of the grim ritual to commence.

"Rayburn," Janus intoned, his voice echoing through the cloistered chamber, "The path to transcendence is fraught with tribulations." His gaze did not falter as he selected a slender, silver instrument, its edge catching the faintest shimmer of magic.

Rayburn braced for what was to come, the promise of power fortifying his spirit. Yet as the first incision carved into his skin, tracing the outer edge of a transmutation circle, a jolt of sharp, unyielding pain lanced through him. His breath hitched, muscles tensing against the relentless cold of steel and sorcery.

The tool danced across Rayburn's back, leaving trails of fiery agony in its wake. Each line drawn by Janus' unwavering hand formed part of a Transmutation circle, a complex web of symbols that pulsed with energy. The pain crescendoed, blossoming into a tortuous symphony, and Rayburn's resolve wavered on the precipice of anguish.

Sweat beaded on Rayburn's brow, mingling with the first drops of blood that now marred his skin. What was once anticipation morphed into a gnawing dread as the true nature of Janus' intentions unveiled itself like a specter raised from forgotten nightmares. These were not merely enhancements; they were shackles forged from his essence, etched into him by a man he revered.

"Master Janus," Rayburn rasped, his voice strained against the onslaught of torment, "is this necessary?" Doubt clouded his heart, a mystery that suffocated the remnants of his boyhood admiration.

"Silence, Rayburn," Janus rebuked without halting his relentless inscription. "Greatness demands sacrifice. Your pain is but a testament to your commitment." His words, once a source of inspiration, now rang hollow amidst the cacophony of Rayburn's unraveling convictions.

As the final stroke cut deep, completing the transmutation circle, Rayburn's vision blurred, tears rolling down his cheeks.

The agony clawed at Rayburn's consciousness as he lay exposed upon the metal table, his back a canvas of raw, bleeding symbols. With each pulse of his heart, a surge of pain radiated from the transmutation circles, each one a brand of Janus' resolve. In the recesses of his mind, a battle raged—a tempest of affection for his mentor contending with the stark revelation of Janus' malevolence.

In that moment of vulnerability, the door to the chamber burst open with a resounding crash. Tomoe stood framed in the threshold, her silhouette a beacon of defiance. Her eyes, wide with shock and brimming with an undeniable clarity, met Rayburn's. They held there, two souls entwined in the silent understanding of the horror before them.

"Rayburn!" Tomoe's voice was a lance, piercing the shroud of despair. "Tomoe..." Rayburn's plea was a mere breath, a flicker of hope amidst the oppressive shadows. Her arrival signified more than companionship; it heralded the dawn of confrontation, the acknowledgment of Janus' unspeakable acts.

As she approached, the truth laid bare in the cold light of the room, Tomoe's features hardened, etched with the sorrow of witnessing a friend's torment and the grim determination to end it. Her sharp eyes, once filled with admiration for the Academy's achievements, now saw only the corruption that festered within its hallowed halls.

"Stop this madness, Janus!" The command resonated through the chamber, a clarion call that shattered the silence. It was a declaration of war against the darkness that had infiltrated the heart of their world.

The tension in the air was palpable, charged with the energy of impending conflict. Janus paused, regarding Tomoe with a gaze as cold and unforgiving as steel. Tomoe's twin blades gleamed ominously in the dim light of the chamber as she stepped forward, her frame a stark contrast to the towering figure of Janus Gravestone. Her eyes, alight with fury and betrayal, locked onto his, demanding accountability without uttering a word.

"Explain yourself, Janus!" Her voice, though soft, cut through the heavy silence like a blade through parchment. "Why are you subjecting Rayburn to such torment? This is not the teachings of the Academy!"

Janus turned his head slowly towards Tomoe, the scars on his face twisting with his grimace. His stance was unwavering, emanating the full weight of his authority and conviction. "Necessity dictates our actions, Tomoe Shinsei," he stated, his tone resolute, echoing around the high stone walls. "The Blindspot threatens us all. Your sentimentality blinds you to the sacrifices required."

"You and your friend's little trifle with the void cost the lives of many dwellers of the Outer Districts. You condemn and judge us in the central for the conditions of the downtrodden; yet your actions changed that existence to ash and blood. Don't get me wrong here, I am not trying to besmirch your efforts, or your noble desires, but nobility demands sacrifices, I bore it in the burdens of Sanctamonium, you now bore them in the cost of lives. But sacrifices and burdens we all have. Rayburn is born with a purpose, many spent their lives looking for one in their meaningless existence, but Rayburn has one, and as heavy as the cross might be, he has to carry it to fruition."

"Your 'sacrifices' reek of cruelty and ambition!" Tomoe retorted, her hair cascading over her shoulders as she bristled with indignation. "There must be another way, one that does not involve mutilating those you claim to protect!"

"Another way?" Janus's laugh was devoid of humor, a chilling sound that reverberated off the ancient stones. "You speak of ideals when the reality of war demands action. I know the path Selene has been guiding you on, friendship and camaraderie, I make the hard choices so that others may live in ignorance of the darkness we combat."

"By plunging us into that very darkness?" Tomoe's accusation hung between them, laden with the weight of unspoken fears. The realization that the man before her was irrevocably lost to his obsessions crystallized in her mind, each word sharpening her resolve.

Janus met her gaze, unflinching. "If it ensures the survival of our world, then yes. I will bear the burden of this darkness." His declaration was final; sealing the rift that had formed within the once-united group.

Rayburn's breath came in ragged gasps, each inhale a dance with agony as the carved symbols on his back pulsed with a sinister heat. His muscles trembled with effort and pain, yet the storm within his dark eyes brewed an unwavering determination. "Enough," Rayburn rasped, his voice a low growl that carried more strength than he felt. With an act of will that seemed to draw upon the cosmos itself, he rose to his feet, swaying slightly as the room blurred at the edges. The transmutation circles etched into his flesh throbbed. "I know, Father. I am but a cheap imitation of the son you once had. His loss still aches deep within both of us. On that day both of us took a solemn promise to see an end to the Darkseiths and free ourselves of the Blindspot. Does a sword cry when its edges shatter against the sword of enemies, does a shield mourn the hits it takes to protect its wielder? I am your sword and shield against the darkness, I am your steel; use me as you see fit."

Tomoe looked at Raymond's faltering stature, his words failing the resolve his words were trying to convey. "Janus," Tomoe addressed the man who towered before her, "you have crossed a line from which there is no return." Her intelligent eyes, so often calm with contemplation, now burned with the fire of defiance. "You speak of necessity, of sacrifice, but this... this is not our way. Your path leads only to ruin,"

Janus's expression hardened further, the lines of his face a map of his unyielding resolve. The chiseled contours of his warrior's visage were set in stone, yet the flicker of something akin to regret passed fleetingly in his eyes—a ghost of what once might have been compassion.

Janus's gaze fell upon Tomoe with the dismissive coldness of a winter's night, his steely eyes betraying not a hint of remorse. "You are but a child, Tomoe," he pronounced, each word dropping like an iron weight. "Your youthful zeal blinds you to the complexities of our world, to the sacrifices that must be made."

Tomoe's lips parted to object, her stance unwavering despite the biting sting of his rebuke. However, it was Rayburn who moved first, his muscles coiling as he rose to his feet. The intricate transmutation circles on his back screamed with fresh agony.

"Enough," Rayburn's voice cut through the thickening air, a blade forged in the fires of his turmoil. His words were directed at Tomoe, but his stormy eyes remained fixed on Janus.

"Rayburn..." Tomoe's voice faltered, the hurt evident in her gaze as she reached out towards him, only to find her efforts repelled by an invisible barrier of his making.

The room seemed to contract around them, the shadows cast by the flickering torchlight grasping at the edges of their silhouettes. Each breath Rayburn drew was laced with the acrid taste of disillusionment.

Janus observed the exchange, his expression unchanging, etched with the resolve of one who has traversed the abyss and returned unscathed. He saw not the defiance in Tomoe's eyes nor the conflict warring within Rayburn; he saw only the necessity of his grand design, his vision unclouded by sentiment.

"Your approval means nothing if it is steeped in darkness," Tomoe whispered.

"Silence," Rayburn commanded again, more forcefully, his heart a drumbeat of internal strife.

"Let her speak, Rayburn," Janus urged, his voice a chilling calm. "The naiveté of youth can be... enlightening."

Tomoe squared her shoulders, ready to unleash the tempest of her resolve, but it was swallowed by Rayburn's conflicted soul. The tension in the room soared, reaching a crescendo that threatened to shatter the fragile truce holding their world together.

"Rayburn," Janus replied, his voice devoid of the warmth once reserved for his protégé. "You must understand."

"Greater good demands greater sacrifices," Janus intoned, his gaze steely.

A drop of blood splattered onto the metallic surface of the table, a crimson testament to the night's work. It spread outwards, a single dark note in the symphony of uncertainty that filled the room. The consequences, as inexorable as the tide, loomed just over the horizon.

Chapter 9

Will and Testament

Seraphim unaware of the events that unfolded in the house of Janus stayed within the academy. He was surrounded by a makeshift council, along with Leandra and Kael awaiting further orders from the Magus Knights or the High Council. The young mage's hands rested firmly on the table before him, fingers splayed wide as if to physically grasp the weight of their tasks ahead of him.

"We cannot sit and wait. Time is not our friend. We have barely a month left before the final attack". Seraphim exclaimed, his voice signifying the storm brewing inside him. The normal calm and composed mage was visually disturbed in the aftermath of the battle in the Outer Sanctum. He could feel the events that would have transpired when his family was wiped out by a similar attack two years ago. Without the help of the mages the first division would have crumbled under the onslaught of the Darkseiths and his family would have perished without even having the chance to defend themselves.

"Then let's not wait around and do what we can". Kael suggested. "We are amidst the ocean of knowledge here, there is no other place to gain knowledge and shine light on the unknown better than the Academy. Let's dive into the bowels of the inner chambers again to check for any information we can find."

With an agreeing nod Leandra continued "we must face the harsh truths of our mission. Do we possess enough knowledge and power to confront this mysterious and otherworldly anomaly known as the Blindspot? The best way to help is to try and unravel any mystery we can."

"Within the Academy's archives lie wealth of knowledge. We have to venture beyond the secret chamber and risk undoing the lock that we had faced before. We know it's a risk but we have to venture forth," came the voice of Tomoe, who had just joined in with Rayburn.

Rayburn had pleaded with Tomoe not to disclose their secret. After much deliberation Tomoe had agreed and it seemed that diving into research was the best way to keep both their mind off the bitter experience.

The notion of delving into the annals of the library sparked a flicker of hope amidst the group's trepidation. The archives were a labyrinthine repository of High Magic's most reclusive secrets.

Seraphim Lumenhart led them, his slender form exuding an aura of steadfast determination as he navigated the labyrinthine corridors with a familiarity born of his regular visits to the chamber. They ventured beyond the secret chamber the trio had discovered before. The doors to what lay beyond were always a mystery as they were unable to figure out the locks. The trio had decided not to test their luck in case the locks were imbued with traps but with time against them, the risks compared to uncovering the knowledge seemed pale. They stood before the archives, a sanctified chamber where knowledge slumbered behind closed doors. It was forbidden to venture into these parts, with expulsion the decided outcome, but now the rewards outweighed any risks. Before them, loomed the entrance, sealed neither by iron nor wood but by a formidable magical barricade. Circular patterns of an intricate seal shimmered across the door's surface, their geometric complexities a challenge only the most adept of mages could hope to decipher.

"Stand clear," intoned Kael, his voice a low thrum that resonated with the power of his convictions. With practiced grace, he extended his hands toward the seal.

While Seraphim focused intently on the seal, Tomoe and Rayburn scoured the nearby shelves. "Anything?" Tomoe's voice was barely above a whisper, her eyes scanning for any tome or trinket that might prove useful.

"Nothing," Rayburn replied, his frustration evident in the response. As he rifled through scrolls and artifacts, his hand brushed against the transmutation circles on his back, a stark reminder that clung to him like a shadow.

The silence between them grew heavy until it was broken by the sound of something soft hitting the floor. Tomoe turned to see Rayburn slumped against the shelf, his face buried in his hands.

"Rayburn?" She moved toward him, her instinct to comfort overtaking her by surprise.

He looked up, and in the dim light, she saw the storm within his dark eyes—a tempest of fear and sorrow that threatened to consume him. "I can't— What if we fail, what if it's all for nothing?" His voice was ragged with emotion, each word laced with the weight of his inner turmoil.

Tomoe reached out, her arms wrapping around him in a gesture that spoke volumes more than words could ever convey. He leaned into the embrace, his body tense as though fighting against the very act of seeking solace.

"Listen to me," she said firmly, her determination lending strength to her voice. "We won't fail. We can't. I believe in you, in us."

His grip tightened around her, and when he spoke again, there was steel in his tone that had been absent moments before. "This is the last time," Rayburn declared, pulling away just enough to look her in the eye. "The last time I show weakness."

Tomoe watched as he composed himself, pushing off from the wall with newfound resolve. As he stood there, his silhouette outlined by the flickering torchlight, she noticed something she hadn't before—the breadth of his shoulders, the stature he carried himself with. Had he always seemed so... formidable?

With a final flourish, the seal's patterns converged, spiraling inward like a galaxy collapsing upon itself. There was a sound, soft as a sigh yet laden with the echo of countless spells unbinding, and with it, the seal dissipated.

A collective breath was drawn as the door swung open with a groan, revealing the vast chamber beyond.

Seraphim wondered why he didn't seek the help of the seniors before; he had a long way to go to catch up to these two formidable figures.

Seraphim's hands shifted over the texts with a reverent touch, seeking any mention of Astolfo or Astaroth in the annals of mythic battles. Each scroll he opened was a potential atlas, leading them closer to the understanding they so desperately sought.

"Focus on anything that speaks of dream magic," he instructed, the urgency in his voice threading through the stillness. "We must find the origin of the Blindspot if we are to stand any chance against it."

Their search was a dance, choreography of necessity as they sifted through the remnants of eras gone by.

"Here, this section is dedicated to heroes of old—Astolfo and Astaroth," Leandra called out.

"By the cosmos," Seraphim whispered, "See here", the group assembling around him. "This might be our key—the way to pierce the veil of the Blind spot's defenses."

Seraphim's fingers traced the ancient script. "The Heart of the Void, within the treacherous depths of the Blindspot," Seraphim continued, his voice steady despite the dread that crept into his blue eyes; "a place where light is devoured by shadow, where the fabric of reality is thin and torn. It might be the focal point of the origin and the key to its destruction. It is a map, of the ancient tome where the ancient council met, where they discussed and decided the fate of the people of the kingdoms. The script overlays the blind spot on top of the map, it shows the geographical center".

The Magus Knights have been trying to figure out the center for ages, but no one could figure out where it started and where it ended. The reconnaissance missions conducted had the main objective of figuring it out. The center holds a lot of significance in a Transmutation circle. The magic forces converge on that point. Maybe it can be used to reverse out the spread. The scroll was hidden among the council documents with maps of different structures; it was so easy to be missed unless it was being specifically sought.

"We need to pass on this information to the Magus Knights and the Council. It is sure to provide a major piece of the puzzle. Leandra you and Kael should be the ones to present this as it were you who figured it out" concluded Seraphim.

"We have already discussed our roles, it you three who deals with the High Council and Magus Knights. We are happy to take a step back in that regard", Kael interrupted, his voice showing signs of distrust which Seraphim wasn't able to place, Rayburn on the other hand couldn't help but notice the shift in the tone, and wonder how much he actually knew about the inner workings of the Magus Knights.

Chapter 10

A Plan Sought through ages.

Janus, Satori, Selene, Mathew, Seraphim, Rayburn and Tomoe were all gathered in the grand hall along with other members of the Ministry and Magus Knights. It was a pivotal point in their strategy. The trio presented their lucky finding to the members, but there was no way to ascertain the validity of the same. The map was created eons past;the landscape had changed over time with dangers lying at every step. There had been earlier missions with Knights venturing into the depths of the Blindspot only to face extreme resistance and casualties, so relying on something with no way of validation could mare their fates with utter failure.

"We have gone through the documents in the archives in detail ones we were made aware of the location of these forgotten relics. The other maps and scriptures found which could have been validated have been done so with utmost accuracy, so based on that, we can also rely on this parchment." Satori bellowed over the ruckus in the hall. His trust on the trio backed his belief on the finding as well.

"That doesn't prove anything. The other parchments that you validated were the ones you wanted to find true. You are leading an investigation with the belief that its correct in the first place, a biased investigation leads to biased results. We have gone through a few documents as well, the history depicted in them are contradictory. The historical events and the turn of events in them do not comply with what we know", Mathew contradicted.

"You are comparing history with geographical maps? History is an account from the sight of the person documenting them, Maps, formulas and scientific facts are not open to interpretation and follow proofs. Our entire society and Magic is based on such ancient documents, how do you refute that?" Satori argued back.

"And how many times have we faced peril due to incorrect transmutation circles, how many lives have been put in jeopardy due to wrong texts? Surely you remember our history and how long it took to filter the scripts and parchments to ensure we have the correct knowledge passing through?" Selene joined in..

It seemed that the discussions would never end. Seraphim was getting annoyed by all the talks and deliberations, Rayburn and Janus were seated calmly as if they expected the meeting to unfold exactly how it was, and Tomoe seemed to be lost within, fighting an invisible battle.

"What choice do we have? What other plan do you have? Instead of going in blind, why can't we trust in what we have in our hands?" Seraphim suddenly burst; his voice a lot louder than he expected. The sudden outburst silenced the entire group, but it was directed towards the council members. "Why don't you come along and test and decide if the parchment hold' true?" the remark was made towards Mathew and his eyes burned with rage at the remark.

As a practice the Ministry council members never ventured out, it was the duty of the Magus Knights. Though it was decided to ensure continuance of government long back, the recent comments from Janus and now from Seraphim intoned a different angle and talked about the cowardice of the council members. Mathew was once part of the Magus Knights and in no way he was ready to listen to a child challenge his valor, but before he could react, Janus stood up and started speaking.

"Young blood boils so fast. You speak of heroics and valor when you haven't even forgotten the taste of childhood, your breath still carries the sweet aroma of milk you drank in your mother's lap. So please excuse the lecture on valor".

Janus's words took Seraphim by surprise, they were too harsh, but he couldn't phantom to cross words with Janus, not on the experiences on the battlefield.

"No one is disagreeing to the contributions made by the older generations, but that doesn't mean we should forget to talk and hold our thoughts, nor does it make every action of them true and turn ours to inaction. The members present shouldn't forget that we were the ones who brought important information from the Eclipse, it was us who defied rules set by you, to keep bringing information time and again, and also, it was us who supported in the recent attack on the outer sanctum which saw the least losses so far. All Seraphim is saying that irrespective of the lack of validation of all the information we need to find a way forward here. Time is not our ally in the upcoming battle and having some sort of a plan is better than having no plan at all…" No one was expecting Tomoe the ever calm and the voice of reason, to have such a strong reaction to Janus, she always revered.

With a smile on his face Janus sat down. "I agree to Tomoe, let us plan ahead, I do have a plan of action, one that can end this entire debacle if the map holds true. But I will need the support of every member, it's not going to be a one man's job, and timing is to be of essence for it to be successful. Especially you Rayburn, I need you by my side the most."

The expression on the faces of Tomoe and Rayburn reflected desperation, but they kept their thoughts to themselves. Seraphim felt the weight of unspoken words, he felt as if there was a secret which lay deep within his friends, their eyes talking tales of a mystery yet to unfold. The final days of the eons old ordeal necessitated camaraderie, yet it seemed the Blindspot had paved its way within the Central, within the hallowed halls of the high council and was making its home within the very hearts of the brave souls who sought to stand against it.

Chapter 11

The Condemned Son

As Rayburn was returning to his room, he saw the messenger Janus used to send whenever he was summoned. A knot began forming in his stomach as he made his way towards the chamber; Janus was already waiting at the doors. The heavy door creaked on its ancient hinges as Janus ushered Rayburn into the chamber—a sanctum of shadows within the heart of the Magus Knights' stronghold. The air was thick, laden with an unspoken promise of what was to come, and it constricted around Rayburn like a tangible force. His steps were measured, echoing softly off the stone floor as he followed his mentor further into the gloom.

Barely perceptible in the dim light, a design of concentric circles began to emerge along the walls. These were the designs of a transmutation circle—the arcane foundation of their order's might, the purpose they served beyond the knowledge of Rayburn.

"Behold," Janus's voice broke through the silence, his tone barely hiding the triumph he felt in presenting a master piece. "The ancient circles, carved from the very essence of the cosmos. Today you shall be complete, transcend mere mages and become the very vessel of deliverance."

As the silence grew heavier, the weight of the impending ritual pressed upon Rayburn, and the transmutation circles seemed to stare back at him, whispering promises of power and portents of doom.

"Rayburn," Janus intoned, "you must serve as the vessel to contain and reverse its malignant tide. The nightmares can be dealt with, can be nullified. The knowledge you and your friends sought can be now used to put an end to the malice of the Blindspot. You have proved to be the rightful brother, and with this, you will prove to be the rightful son."

Janus's eyes, twin beacons of resolve, bore into Rayburn with an intensity that bordered on ferocity. The sacred duty bestowed upon him by the man who was both his mentor and tormentor weighed heavily upon Rayburn's spirit, yet he stood resolute.

Rayburn's gaze locked onto Janus, whose presence loomed over him like a tempest on the cusp of eruption. In the shadowy flicker of candlelight, the stark lines of resolve etched across the older man's face were as pronounced as the ancient symbols adorning the walls. There was a fervor in Janus's eyes—a steadfastness born of desperate necessity.

Janus's hand emerged from the folds of his robe, grasping ablack blade with an edge that mirrored the night itself. Rayburn felt the sharp intake of breath that wasn't entirely his own; even the room seemed to hold its breath, the silence punctuated only by the soft whistle of the blade slicing through the air as Janus raised it.

The first touch of the blade against his skin was a shock more than a pain—a cold, hard declaration that there was no turning back. But then the carving began, and the true agony followed. Each incision was a fiery brand, a torturous dance of blade against flesh that dragged screams from the depths of Rayburn's throat to be trapped behind clenched teeth. Each stroke was precise, Janus's hands never faltering, as if guided by a will beyond human frailty. The scent of iron filled the air, and Rayburn could feel the transmutation circles taking shape, each one a link in the chain that would bind him to the magic.

With every line carved, Rayburn's consciousness teetered on the brink. His mind recoiled, seeking refuge in memories of the Central's cobblestone streets under moonlight, or Tomoe's comforting presence. Yet those solaces crumbled beneath the relentless tide of suffering that now defined his existence. Bound by duty and honed by torment, Rayburn endured.

The chamber echoed with the sounds of Rayburn's muffled agony, a chorus underscored by the drip of his own blood. He could feel the eyes of his mentor upon him, those piercing orbs that had seen battles untold and bore witness to the rise and fall of countless Magus Knights. Yet now, they shone with fervor that bordered on the divine, or perhaps the infernal. A silent scream clawed its way through his throat, as the design began to take shape.

Janus, his voice unwavering, continued to channel the sinister energies, his hands raised as if sculpting the very air around them. Twisted shadows danced along the chamber walls with the flickering torches, as if averting their eyes to the macabre scene. Within their eerie light, Rayburn's form appeared both divine and monstrous—an avatar of untold potential birthed from darkness and despair.

The ritual reached its zenith, and for a fleeting moment, there was a palpable stillness, as if time itself held its breath. Janus, his expression a complex tapestry of victory and sorrow, watched as the man he considered his son emerged anew, forged in the crucible of forbidden sorcery.

"Forgive me," Janus murmured, his voice barely more than a whisper lost energy that filled the chamber and then everything fell silent, as if time itself had stopped in tracks.

The sudden silence was deafening.

Rayburn's eyes, glazed with torment, flickered in the dimming light, reflecting a mosaic of emotions. Betrayal gnawed at his insides, a bitter poison that mingled with the remnants of filial devotion. The duality of his gaze, caught between reverence and revulsion for the man who had raised him, mirrored the duality of the world he inhabited—the stark contrast of light and darkness.

In that silence, broken only by the labored breathing of the wounded, the line between heroism and sacrifice blurred. And in the ghostly afterglow of the ritual's passing, Rayburn's tortured form was not merely a reminder of what had been lost—but also of what remained to be fought for.

Chapter 12

Impossible Choices

Emergency summons went across from the stronghold of the Magus Knights. The leaders of the Magus Knights and the Academy were summoned in the middle of the night with the message that a solution had been found. It was the breakthrough that everybody was looking for, with the ides of March just breaths away. Finally it seemed all the pieces were in place and instead of a desperate attempt, their attack could derive the results the Sanctamonium longed for. But the scene in the chamber where everyone was summoned unfolded a dark chapter in the history of mages.

The chamber's air, thick with shadows and the scent of ancient stone, shivered as Seraphim paced its perimeter. In its center was Rayburn Wilder, convulsed on the cold floor, his form wracked by spasms of unspeakable pain. Seraphim halted, his piercing gaze fixed on Rayburn's contorted figure. The once-stoic warrior's back, now bared to the observing eyes, bore the unmistakable etchings of transmutation circles. Each mark seared into Rayburn's skin was a dark testament to forbidden rituals, the blood-ink used to inscribe them still fresh. His face, a canvas of torment, twisted in an anguished.

Beside the fallen knight knelt Tomoe Shinsei, her arms wrapped tightly around him in a desperate embrace. Her tear-streaked face nestled close to his, offering silent comfort amidst the chaos. Crystal droplets born of grief and helplessness trickled down her cheeks, each one a silent witness to the depth of her connection to Rayburn. Her twin blades lay discarded beside her, their lethal beauty forgotten in the face of the raw humanity unfolding within the chamber's confining walls.

The other Magus Knights stood as sentinels at the periphery, their expressions a mixture of concern and wary anticipation. They each knew the gravity of what unfolded before them. Satori stared in disbelief as if in a dream, the very ground on which he stood had been replaced with a slippery slope he was struggling to stand upon. Janus was his mentor, his brother in arms; he had himself seen the depths of love he had for his children, yet his obsession had turned him into a creature of the darkness. No matter how noble the thought or the weightage on the final outcome, Janus harming his children was unfathomable.

The other Magus Knights present though seemed to accept the fate written for Rayburn, they had seen countless lives lost for a singular cause, a little disfigurement was of no consequence to them. They were so focused in the outcome and their belief and their cause, that to them the pain and suffering a few didn't even register. Most of the higher Magus Knights belonged to the renowned Magus families, and to them Rayburn was still an orphan of the Outer Sanctum, who didn't deserve the grace Janus had bestowed and this was a way he can repay some of the debt he had accrued by using his name and the Gravestone crest he adorned.

"What have they done to you?" Seraphim whispered the words scarcely audible over Rayburn's moans. His mind grappled with the sight, the transmutation circles on Rayburn's back a grotesque mockery of their sacred magic, of everything he believed in. This was no mere application of their art; it was a perversion, a corruption that clawed at the very fabric of their brotherhood.

He clenched his fists, the knuckles whitening as he fought against the impulse to scream, to demand answers from the man who he considered his hero. His gaze shifted to his fellow Magus Knights, searching their faces for some semblance of guidance, only to find reflections of approval and the stark difference between the Sanctums became as prominent as the walls that divided them.

It was Tomoe's anguished cry that shattered the suffocating silence. "Janus!" Her voice crackled with the fire of her rage. She rose trembling with the force of her emotions as she confronted their leader. "What have you wrought upon him? Speak!"

Janus Gravestone turned slowly to face her, his stern visage betraying no hint of remorse."Explanations are owed, yes, but not here," he said, his voice striking like flint.

"Here and now, Janus!" Tomoe insisted, stepping closer. "You owe us all the truth. What darkness have you invited into Rayburn's flesh?"

"I would have with held the discussions till a council meeting but since you are impatient let me tell you the truth. The Blindspot, Obscura Umbra, Great Divide, call it by whatever name you can imagine, is nothing but the after effects of our magic. We say we use dream space, but dreams also are filled with nightmares. It is where our fears take shape and has the power to send shivers across our spine. We wake up and forget about these dreams and sigh a relief that it was just a nightmare, but imagine a world where these nightmares come true. That's your Blindspot."

As the group listened to the revelations in horror trying to grasp the meaning behind, Janus continued. "We use dream energy for our magic but our transmutation circles leave out the dark magic from the nightmares. It's really simple actually had any of the scores of magus tried to understand how magic works in this realm, instead of trying to defeat an unknown force. The only missionswe sent our Knights out for, were to identify the centre of the Blindspot, and now we have that information. We can reverse the magic and confine it, and now we have a vessel to do just that."

"Enough!" Seraphim's voice cut through the confrontation, resolute and clear. "We cannot allow our purpose to be lost in shadow. Our path must be one of light, or we forsake all we stand for."

All eyes turned to Seraphim.

Janus stood firm, a monolith of resolve amidst the tempest of emotions swirling through the chamber. His voice, a bastion of unwavering certainty, resonated against the cold stone walls as he defended his deeds.

"Sanctamonium demands sacrifice," Janus declared, his face devoid of remorse. "The transmutations upon Rayburn are but a necessity."

"Your 'necessary sacrifices' scream of betrayal!" Tomoe retorted. "How does inflicting pain serve the greater good?"

Tension coiled in the air, a tangible force that threatened to erupt into chaos with each exchanged word. The Magus Knights still held their ground and kept their thoughts to themselves awaiting an outcome, for arguments aside and beyond good and evil, there was a needfor a new dawn to Sanctamonium's thousand year night.

"Silence your doubts, Tomoe," Janus commanded, his stoic mask slipping ever so slightly to reveal a glint of fervor. "What is one life weighed against the future of all Sanctamonium? I have seen the edge of oblivion; darkness ebbs at our doorstep!"

"Darkness? Or is it your own shadow we see, stretching over us all?" Tomoe pressed, her voice rising to meet Janus's with equal force. Her accusation sliced through any pretense of respect that once existed between master and apprentice.

The other knights shifted uncomfortably, the weight of loyalty and conscience pressing down upon them. As Tomoe and Janus's voices crescendoed into a cacophony of discord, the very essence of their mission seemed to hang precariously in balance.

The chamber's air lay thick with acrid tension, a suffocating cloak that seemed to taint each drawn breath.

Within the confines of this forbidding space, Seraphim stood motionless, his gaze locked onto the writhing form of Rayburn. The anguished cries that had once filled the room now echoed only in the hollow silence of his mind, where a tempest of doubt and fear raged.

As Tomoe's impassioned pleas and Janus's cold retorts faded into the periphery of his consciousness, Seraphim turned inward, confronting the shadow that loomed within his own heart. He had been a steadfast beacon of hope, devoted to sanctifying Sanctamonium through the purity of magic. But what purity remained when their most sacred rites inflicted suffering on one of their own?

"Is this the justice we wield?" Seraphim murmured to himself, his voice barely a thread in the oppressive silence. "Have we become so blinded by our quest that we forsake our humanity?"

No longer could he stand idle as a silent witness to the erosion of their noble cause. The weight of decision anchored his resolve, a newfound defiance kindling within his chest. It was time to challenge Janus, to hold firm against the creeping darkness that sought to claim them all.

"Janus," he spoke, his tone resolute, every word imbued with the gravity of his intent. "I will not follow you down this path. We must find another way."His challenge hung in the air, Seraphim braced for the fallout, ready to weather the storm he had summoned; the fate of Rayburn, and perhaps all of Sanctamonium, hinged on what would unfold next.

Janus turned slowly, his presence imposing as ever, the scars of his past battles etched deep within his stony visage. His eyes, usually so piercing and commanding, now simmered with a barely contained fury.

"Defiance," Janus said, the word seething between clenched teeth. "You challenge me? After all I have done for you? For Sanctamonium?"

His heavy boots grounded him firmly, as if he drew power from the very stones beneath. The air seemed to thicken around him, charged with the latent energy of his anger.

"Your path leads to our ruin, Janus," Seraphim pressed on

"Sanctamonium demands sacrifice!" Janus roared again, his voice booming against the chamber walls. "Do you not see the Blindspot encroaching? Will you cower behind sentiment while our world crumbles?"

But Seraphim held his ground, his resolve unshaken. In his stance, there was a defiance born not of arrogance but of a profound belief in a greater good—a vision that transcended the narrow confines of Janus's dogma.

"Then let it be my sacrifice," Seraphim offered, his tone sober.

For a moment, the chamber fell silent, the echoes of their confrontation hanging heavy in the air. Janus's expression twisted into a mask of frustration, the lines of his face deepening as the realization set in—his grip on the

Magus Knights was faltering, his absolute authority cracking under the strain of Seraphim's conviction.

And in the quiet that followed, the balance of power shifted imperceptibly, like the first subtle turn of the seasons, heralding a change that none could yet fathom.

"Okay, then you be the sacrifice. How do you plan to attack the heart of the Blindspot with the Darkseith's onslaught? Talks are all fine, and magnanimous ideals are fine, but how are you going to win?"

The question hung in the air. The chamber's air crackled with tension, thick and palpable as the aftermath of a thunderclap. Seraphim's challenge to Janus had been a fissure in the once-solid foundation of their order.

"We will attack in a two pronged approach, one will be a distraction to lure the Darkseiths, I will lead the same and the other a tactical team to pierce the heart of the Blindspot". Satoriwhisperedwith defiance in his voice. He knew the diversion would be met with heavy losses.

"Victory demands sacrifices", said Janus. "But how will that end the Blindspot? With your immense knowledge on the subject, how do you plan to stop the onslaught?" Janus didn't even attempt to mask the sarcasm in his voice. There is only one way forward, only one chance to put an end to this age old misery, to repay our debts to all who sacrificed before us. Your morals are not going to forge the path forward, you know as much as I do. You should consider yourself lucky that I chose my own son for this ordeal, I could have very well chosen you or any of your children to be sacrificed for the future of the Sanctums."

"Why didn't you choose yourself?" Tomoe retorted. "Why make your son suffer, why not be the vessel yourself?"

"Each of us has a role to play," replied Janus swiftly, his voice reflecting his annoyance with this discussion rather than a hurry to answer the question. "While in the center of the Blindspot, what kind of creatures do you think you will face? It was Satori and I who defeated the Vicar hiding in the shadows on the day of the attack of the Outer Sanctum, which stopped the onslaught, the very battle you keep reminding us of. Do you think if a Vicar or a Sin appeared, there are others who can stop them from ending the ritual? Satori bravely volunteered to lead the main forces, but what about the tactical force? Who is going to defend them right at the center?"

Silent fell in the room; no one had a retort to his question. Janus had planned every step like he did on every mission before; the Magus Knights knew questioning their leader was futile.

Janus's departure was not silent; it thundered through the chamber with the fury of a tempest. Each footfall resounded, an ominous drumbeat that marked the fracturing of bonds once thought unbreakable. The heavy door slammed shut behind him, and the echoes reverberated like the final tolls of a death knell for unity among the Magus Knights.

The dimly lit chamber seemed to contract in the wake of his exit, shadows creeping along the walls as if drawn by the vacuum left by his formidable presence. The remaining Magus Knights lingered in a silence that was almost palpable, each lost in the tumult of their thoughts, their loyalties cleaved in twain by the sharp edge of conflict.

Seraphim stood statue-like, his gaze fixed on the closed door. The air crackled with the tension of unspoken fears and unasked questions. It was as if the act of Janus Gravestone, their leader, had written anew the fabric of their reality, leaving them adrift in a sea of doubt.

Chapter 13

Call to Arms

Back at the academy, Seraphim and Tomoe told the group about what transpired in the meeting. The reality of Blindspot as disclosed by Janus and what happened to Rayburn. Rayburn stood at the corner, resting on the wall while the revelations brought about different emotions from the group. The chamber echoed with the clangor of heated discourse, an alchemical mix of fear and resolve simmering in each utterance.

Students are mere kids, their world divided in black and white. There is good and evil and the lines between them well defined. As one grows up the lines start to fade and a grey area emerge. Over time it's the grey people live in. Leandra and Kael being the seniors knew the blurry lines well; perhaps among the students in the Academy, they were the ones who could feel the logic behind Janus's actions.

"Darkseiths encroach upon every boundary, and here we stand, quarreling like children!" Leandra Skylark's voice cut through the din, her frustration palpable as she slammed a fist against the ancient oak table around which they gathered.

"Leandra is right," another chimed in, "We've seen what lies beyond the Blindspot. Not one of us can claim certainty in facing what awaits."

"Can I?" The question slipped from Seraphim's lips before he could tether it, a whisper barely louder than a thought.

"Seraphim?" said a mage near the window, her voice tinged with concern. "We have always spoken openly among ourselves. Don't falter now."

"Perhaps not as individuals, but together..." He paused, grappling with the self-doubt that clawed at his conviction."Sanctamonium demands more of us, it calls for unity, for a collective might greater than any individual fear. We are nothing without each other, without each other's courage or resolve. We have been brought together by a cause, and that end still holds true."

"Friends," Tomoe began, her voice a soft whisper, "we are surrounded on all sides by doubt and darkness. But we must not forget the light we have kindled together, the victories we have won were no mere happenstance; they were born of our unity, our shared strength."

Leandra echoed Tomoe's sentiment with a nod. "Aye," she agreed, her voice imbued with a resonance that belied her graceful form. "We have weathered storms aplenty. Each challenge surmounted has prepared us for this moment—the Blindspot shall be no different."

Her laughter, though tinged with the gravity of their situation, rippled through the chamber, disarming the tension that had bound them. The tension seemed to dissipate, uniting the group ones more, focusing on the battle ahead.

Rayburn's voice was a deep echo from a well of unseen depth. "I've seen what lies within the Blindspot, the maddening void. I'm still terrified from my last encounter and I understand the feeling dwelling inside all of you, but persist we must."

"You spoke a little too late Rayburn, Leandra had already lifted our spirits," commented Kael with a hint of laughter in his voice. "Remember the markets of the Outer Districts the day after the Darkseiths came. Do you recall how the people rebuilt? How they took up their tools with hands trembling but determined, hearts laden with loss but unbeaten?"

A collective breath was drawn, and within the exhalation laid a shared epiphany. In the aftermath of destruction, there had been rebirth—an undeniable testament to the resilience of humanity. It was a moment of triumph, not of grandeur or spectacle, but of simple, profound courage.

"Such is our power," Seraphim declared, his words resounding with newfound vigor; "the strength to rise, to mend what has been torn asunder. This Blindspotseeks to unravel us—but we shall weave our fate anew."

It was the night before the final attack, the next day was to bring in a new dawn, or it was going to bring forth nightmares the likes of which no one had ever fathomed.

Chapter 14

The Last Stand

The core of Sanctamonium throbbed with a palpable tension, the fortress-city braced in anticipation. The Magus Knights started their march from the heart of the City, the second division joining in from the second Sanctum. Seraphim and the students followed as part of the Third division. The streets were lined with the citizens gathered to spectacle a march like never before. Its felt that the ground shook beneath their fleets as the convoy marched on. The children cheered on,encouraging the troops set to bring about a new dawn in the history of the Sanctamonium.

As the group gathered near the Outer Sanctum facing the void in front of them the mood started to shift. The energy and optimism started to fade and was slowly being overtaken by anxiety and pessimism.

"Magus Knights, Soldiers and the students of Academia Magorum" Janus's voice cut through the silence, as steady as the stone walls that cradled them."This confrontation with the Darkseiths is inevitable. Their malignant whispers have breached our dreams, seeking to fracture our unity. But we stand here today as one. Today there are no inner and outer Sanctums, no ranks and divisions among you based on your magical affinity, no class or creed. We stand as a force united against the might of the darkness before us, and we will be triumphant."

He paused, allowing his gaze to affirm the importance of every soul present. "Our strategy relies not just on the might of our spells, but on the strength of our bond. Each of you possesses abilities wrought from the very cosmos. Today, we weave our powers into a single force, one that will hold steadfast against the tide of oblivion. Alone, we are formidable. Together, we are invincible. We fight not only for Sanctamonium, but for the dreams of all those who dwell within its walls—from the affluent heights of the Central to the hardy souls of the Outer Districts. So let us go forth and steal this victory from the clutches of the fate which put us here. Let us be a force, whose light shines so bright, that the Blindspot ceases from its existence ones and for all."

The forces shouted in unison and all doubts were destroyed in its echo. It was a declaration of war directed towards all that lay within the Blindspot.

The Strategy for the upcoming battle was laid out by Janus and Satori the day before. Mathew and Selene of the High council couldn't do much but agree. The forces are to be divided into two factions. First, the diversionary forces, was to attack head on. The recent spout between Seraphim and Janus rewarded Seraphim in the way of making him the second in command after Satori to lead the forces. High Casualty was expected if the plan is to be successful, and the blunt would be faced by both of them.

Second, would be a tactical unit, comprising of Janus himself, Rayburn, Tomoe (she refused to leave Rayburn's side) and five of the trusted Magus Knights and acolytes of Janus. Each of the five was to hold a specific position in the center of the Blindspot, with Rayburn at the very center. Janus and Tomoe would be warding off any residual Darkseiths once everyone was in position. It was assured by Janus that no harm would come to Rayburn or any of the acolytes, in the sense that they weren't sacrificial lambs.

The acrid scent of scorched earth clawed through the air as the boots slid across the charred ground on the outskirts of the Blindspot. As their eyes began adjusting to the darkness, they were faced with an army of Darkseiths clawing their way towards the city's vulnerable fringe.

"Kael!" Seraphim shouted, his voice cutting through the cacophony of battle. Kael charged ahead as he deflected an onslaught of shadowed claws with a barrier woven of dream energy. Beside him, Leandra danced through the chaos, her lithe form cutting a swath through the encroaching Darkseiths.

"Form up!" Seraphim commanded, his tone brooking no argument. "We cannot let them stop us!"

Around him, the defenders rallied, their morale bolstered by his unwavering presence. He moved with calculated precision, positioning soldiers and mages alike, orchestrating their movements as if they were pieces on a grand chessboard. His strategy unfolded in real-time, as each member of his impromptu militia found their place in his plan. The strategy was different this time around, with the mages leading and the first division laying back o take care of any remaining Darkseiths. The aim was to save as many as possible.

"Leandra, reinforce the eastern flank. They're pressing hard there," Seraphim directed, his gaze never leaving the surging tide of Darkseiths. Her nod was brisk, her movements already a blur as she summoned barriers of incandescent energy.

"Kael, you hold the center. Your magic is strongest there." Seraphim's own hands weaved intricate patterns in the air, summoning forth bolts of radiant energy that scythed through the masses of creatures with surgical precision.

"Understood," came Kael's terse reply, his expression grim yet determined. Each new wave of Darkseiths crashed against their fortifications, only to be repelled by the combined might of their arcane prowess and the steely resolve of those who fought beside them.

"Keep them at bay!" Seraphim called out, his voice resonating with the authority of a born leader.

The air crackled with the scent of magic and charred flesh, filled by the cacophony of battle cries and the sinister hisses of the Darkseiths. Kael stood firm in the eye of the storm, his dark eyes scanning the battlefield as he prepared to unleash his might upon the encroaching horde, a beacon of hope amidst the chaos.

The battle raged on—a tornado of magic and malice, with the fate of a city hanging precariously in the balance. The forces pressed on inside the Blindspot, holding their tight formation, gaining an inch at a time.

On the other side Satori lead his troops. His blades cutting through the Darkseiths like a hot blade across butter. His moves were gaining ground and providing courage to the ones who followed.

Without warning the ground shook, and from the writhing mass of Darkseiths emerged a new abomination that dwarfed its brethren both in size and malice. It was a Vicar much bigger than the one Satori faced in the Eclipse. Towering above the fray, its form was an amalgamation of nightmares—a grotesque mockery of life. Its hide was thick like an armor, impervious to mundane weapons, its claws sharp and long, seeking the life force of anything they touched.

The newly arrived fiend was Satori's group to contend with, and time was not their ally. "By the light that shines upon everything, cleanse. Come forth the shadows from the abyss" he intoned, his voice carrying the resonance of amage. Arcane sigils flared to life around him, casting eerie shadows on the broken ground. In his hands came into life twin orbs of destructive energy—one of roiling darkness, the other of searing light—each a testament to his mastery over the conflicting forces. The orbs engulfed his twin swords, each hand holding a destructive force.

With a calculated gaze, he attacked the monstrosity, knowing that only precise strikes at its core could hope to breach its formidable defenses. He conserved his magical reserves carefully, for each spell cast was a draught drawn from a well that could run dry all too soon.

As the attacks cut through the behemoth, a thunderous explosion shook the battlefield. Shadows and light danced wildly, intertwining in a deadly dance that seemed to stretch the fabric of reality itself. For a moment, it appeared as though the creature faltered, its form buckling under the onslaught of Satori's power. Yet even as hope flickered amongst the ranks of Sanctamonium's defenders, the beast reeled back with an ear-splitting screech, unbroken and undeterred, its malevolence undiminished.

A sudden shift in the winds of magic drew Leandra's attention to the periphery. Kael, a figure of determined strength, had become isolated from the group, his focus solely on the Darkseith before him. His magic surged, yet even he could not keep the swarm at bay indefinitely. The lesser creatures, emboldened by the distraction, converged upon him with bloodthirsty glee. Leandra swiftly reached for support.

Without a faltering step, Satori continued with his onslaught, attack after attack from his twin blades cutting deep into the enemy until finally it fell down with a giant thud on the ground. The lesser Darkseiths and the soldiers around Satori were enchanted by the ongoing duel, still on their tracks, awaiting the victor to emerge. As the behemoth fell, enthusiastic battle cries and terrifying shrieks filled the air in unison.

The duel had taken its toll on Satori as he had spent more magic than he expected. He was nearly depleted when he was joined by his allies a little too late. They stood as walls against the onslaught and yet the attacks made their mark on him. Injured and bleeding, he pressed on, spells flew, steel sang, and slowly, inch by hard-fought inch, the Darkseiths were driven back from their quarry.

But the fight was far from over, the clamor of battle rose to a feverish pitch as Seraphim, Kael, and Leandra faced the relentless waves of Darkseiths that surged toward them like a tide of malice. Their forms, grotesque parodies of life's natural grace, threw themselves against the barriers woven from arcane energy and cold steel.

Seraphim's slender frame bore the brunt of the assault, his blade moving with perfect precision. Sweat beaded on his brow, the strain evident in the tightness of his jaw and the grim set of his lips. The pain of exertion lanced through his muscles, but he dared not falter. He was so focused on the next move, the next attack, that there was no space for doubt or to think beyond.

"Push them back!" he commanded, though his voice was hoarse from shouting over the din of combat. "We cannot let them—"

But his words were cut short as a new breed of Darkseith, massive and pulsing with an ominous power, burst through the line. Its presence sowed chaos, disrupting the harmony of their defense. It bore down upon them with a speed that belied its size, and for a moment, the very air seemed to tremble.

Kael's dark hair clinging to his sweat-drenched forehead as he raised his hands and unleashed a barrage of spells, the raw power of his Mage class abilities manifesting as bolts of lightning and orbs of fire. Yet his stormy eyes betrayed his caution, his every move conserving energy for the battle that still raged beyond this moment.

"Leandra!" Kael's voice cracked under the strain as he saw her petite form flung aside by the sheer force of the new Darkseith's advance.

She rolled to her feet, her blade ready, and her expression unreadable save for the sharp focus in her intelligent eyes. Despite the terror this new foe inspired, her calm never wavered; it was the rock upon which the tide of darkness broke. With a deft motion, she summoned another barrier.

For a time, it seemed they might hold the line. But the Darkseiths were tireless, their hunger undiminished by loss or pain. As one fell, two more took its place, and the defenders' energy waned. A crack appeared in their formation, and through it, the creatures poured.

"Fall back!" Seraphim's command sliced through carrying with it the weight of the decision. It was a retreat, a concession that gnawed at their pride. They moved as one, retreating step by grueling step, leaving the ground littered with the bodies of their foes. Their breaths were ragged, their movements sluggish with fatigue, yet there wasn't a moment of respite.

As they reached the safety of the sanctum's walls, the echo of their flight followed them, a reminder of the defense they had abandoned. Leandra's gaze met Seraphim's, and in that silent exchange lay the burden of leadership and the cost of war.

"What hope have we against such odds?" came a voice from one of the troops.

"Hope is not lost while we yet stand," Kael replied, his voice steely as he prepared to unleash another barrage of spells.

"Regroup," instructed Seraphim.

Meanwhile, Janus, Rayburn and Tomoe along with a few of the Magus Knights made their way deep into the Blindspot.

As they drew near the center, the Darkseiths converged, eager to crush this newfound threat. But Janus's intellect, honed by years of study and sharpened by necessity, proved their undoing. The tactics of his foes were laid bare before him, he anticipated their every move, weaving between strikes with preternatural grace.

Rayburn Wilder moved among his brethren, a specter cloaked in darkness, yet alight with the fire of purpose. His transmutation circles hummed with forbidden power, etched into his flesh, the pain of their creation was a distant echo now, drowned out by the cacophony of clashing steel and shattering incantations.

"Stay the course!" Janus's voice cut through the commotion, as much a beacon as any spell of light could hope to be.

A shimmering barrier, wrought from the collective will of his allies, shielded them from a volley of poisoned shadows. It was Tomoe's doing, her twin blades slicing through the air, carving runes that breathed life into their defense. She cast a glance toward Rayburn, a silent promise echoing in the steel of her gaze.

"Your time is now, Ray," she whispered, words meant only for him, carried on the winds of war.

Each Acolyte took his position around Rayburn, forming a star, points within a circle. Janus and Tomoe took positions to defend the group from any onslaught, but the ruckus at the fronts distracted the Darkseiths, the plan of Janus coming to fruition. As Rayburn channeled the dreams of eons into the transmutation circles that splayed across his back, they glowed, a sigil of defiance against the night. The Acolytes started their silent incantations, each with a pair of their own transmutation circles etched on each of their arms.

As the glow became brighter, Tomoe could feel a shift in the atmosphere. It was as if the air was becoming lighter, the gloom vanishing and the light from the transmutation circles flowing through her with the familiar warmth of Rayburn. She felt wave after wave of energy flowing through the space, each washing away everything sinister around.

The Darkseiths' leader, recognizing the shift in tactics, bared its fangs in a grotesque semblance of a smile. He rushed towards the center to finish off the epicenter of the ripples spreading across.

"Let me handle it, you focus on keeping Ray safe," shouted Janus. Tomoe nodded, feeling the power within him swell like a storm-tossed sea. He fixed his dark eyes upon the Darkseiths' leader, a monstrous creature of malice that towered over the battlefield, commanding its horde with guttural roars. The ground shook under the weight of his conviction as he passed through the melee, untouched by claw or spell. The name "Sin", the reference to the leader of the Darkseiths proved rightly so.

With a cry that melded rage and triumph, Janus unleashed his pent-up magic. Dark tendrils erupted from his hands, writhing serpents of pure void that hungered for the corruption they faced. The leader of the Darkseiths reared back, its confidence shattered as the dark magic met its flesh, tearing at the essence of its being.

The beast let out an anguished bellow, its form buckling under the onslaught. A shockwave of dark energy pulsed outward, knocking lesser creatures aside as if they were mere playthings.

And then, silence fell—a brief respite, punctuated by the ragged breaths of Janus and Tomoe and the thud of the Darkseiths' leader collapsing to the earth.

The ritual Rayburn was at the center of wasn't at its end yet, as the transmutation circles glowed brighter still. And then a sudden thump, reeled all the darkness towards

Rayburn. It was as if the Blindspot was collapsing into itself. Rayburn was lifted off the ground, Tomoe, Janus and the Acolytes barely holding their positions, as dust and ash swept through with the encroaching darkness, finding its way towards Rayburn. And in a split second it was over.

The Magus Knights hesitated, scarcely able to believe the turn of events. But there, standing amidst the turmoil, was Rayburn Wilder, his body aglow with the remnants of his power, the harbinger of dawn in a world besieged by night.

In the wake of Janus's cataclysmic ritual, the battlefield before Sanctamonium transformed into a tableau of victory and exhaustion; Darkseiths, their will to fight severed as decisively as their leader had been, recoiled from the aftermath, their forms dissolving into shadow. The air, once thick with the stench of malevolence, now palpitated with the euphoria of survival.

Seraphim Lumenhart stood at the forefront, his slender frame silhouetted against the dwindling chaos, blue eyes reflecting the somber glow of twilight. His robes bore the marks of battle, yet he emanated an unyielding authority, a beacon amidst the encroaching gloom. Around him, his brethren-in-arms regrouped; their figures haggard but undefeated, each face etched with relief that mirrored his own. "We hold the line." His gaze swept across his comrades, seeing not just the warriors who had banded together under his command but the shared dream they all protected—a Sanctamonium that could breathe free of fear.

Rayburn himself, the architect of their triumph, seemed to teeter on the edge of collapse, dark magic clinging to his form like a lover's embrace. He leaned heavily on his enchanted weapon, its glow dimming as the final vestiges of energy ebbed away. Yet his dark eyes remained vigilant, scanning the darkness for any sign of resurgence, ready to defend until his very last breath.

Above, the cosmos pulsed, its celestial dance undisturbed by the mortal conflict below. It was within that vast expanse that the source of their magic lay—dreams interwoven with the fabric of the multiverse, granting them powers both wondrous and terrible. The planetary convergence had amplified their abilities beyond measure, yet it was their unity and indomitable spirit that had carried the day.

Satori, beaten and tattered, yet not broken, looked up at the sky, as the faint light started to seep in. Janus's plan had worked, his years of knowledge and relentless pursuit finally paid off and not a moment too late. Leandra looked at Kael, her eyes holding back her tears, a day they didn't dare to imagine had come to pass, Kael passed his reassuring smile, blood dripping from his forehead.

The tension that had gripped the battlefield began to dissipate, replaced by the profound relief of survival and the silent acknowledgment of sacrifices made. The Magus Knights, though battered and bruised, radiated a sense of invincibility that stemmed not from arrogance but from a bond forged in the crucible of war—a unity unbreakable even in the face of formidable adversaries.

Chapter 15

The Everlasting Dawn

The battlefield a testament of violence, the air thick with the scent of charred earth and the metallic tang of spilled blood. The clamor of steel rang out as Magus Knights clashed with the final remnants of the Darkseiths.

In the heart of this chaos stood Rayburn Wilder, his form a lone bastion amidst the storm. Across from him loomed Janus Gravestone, an imposing figure against the backdrop of battle-scarred terrain. Between them stretched a distance of a few paces, yet it spanned over eons, the silence louder than the sounds of the battle around.

Rayburn's gaze locked onto Janus, twin pools of darkness reflecting an inner tempest. Within his chest, the heartbeat of dark magic pulsed, a sinister rhythm that threatened to consume his very being. His hands trembled, not from fear, but from the effort to contain the power coursing through him. "Focus," he whispered to himself, the word barely audible.

He was brimming with darkness, filled with memories he kept his best to keep at bay. His childhood memories, where he was tortured and bullied, his helplessness at the loss of his brother, his torment at the hands of his father. With each thought his heart and mind was being ravished with a rage he didn't feel before. His tattered body had left his mark on his soul, which seemed to be crumbling with every passing thought, all the focus of his hatred slowly being directed towards Janus.

He was the eye of the storm, the wielder of nightmares, standing ready to confront the twisted ambition of Janus Gravestone. And though his body quaked with the effort, with a surge of will, Rayburn directed the darkness, shaping it into a weapon against the man who had once been his mentor, his father in all but blood.

Janus Gravestone lunged with the ferocity of a seasoned warrior, his blade a silver arc slicing through the attacks. Sparks danced upon contact, a shower of celestial fire born from the collision of metal.

The Acolytes sprang into action, to defend their master lunging towards Rayburn. Before she knew it, Tomoe's body moved in defense, becoming a wall between the acolytes and him.

As the darkness of the Blindspot slowly dissipated, another better raged at its peak.

The tide turned as Rayburn tapped into the dual wellsprings of his power, the darkness within him coalescing with the elemental forces at his command. He summoned forth streams of water that leaped from his fingertips, each spell interwoven with the tendrils of shadow magic. Water spiraled into lashing whips, all commanded by the arcane choreography of warlock and mage combined.

A flicker of awe, then fear, crept into Janus' eyes as he witnessed the breadth of Rayburn's might, a power that transcended mere ambition. The elder's precision gave way to desperation, his relentless assault faltering under the onslaught of elemental fury and creeping darkness. Janus, who had once stood as an unmovable monolith in the face of danger, now faced the realization that his own creation outstripped him in mastery of magic.

In this dance of destruction, Rayburn moved with the grace of inevitability, his formal attire swirling about him like the mantle of fate itself. Each gesture wove another layer of spell work, his words incantations of a reality shaped by his will. The battlefield bore witness to the emergence of a force that defied the simple boundaries of magic, one wrapped in the guise of a man who had been forged by his own nightmares.

Even as his body screamed in protest, the scars on Rayburn's back burning, his mind remained clear and focused. It was more than a battle for survival; it was an assertion of his very identity amidst the fractured reflections of love and hatred that painted his soul in shades darker than any spell could conjure.

"Janus!" Their gazes locked, two storms colliding in the silence that punctuated the clamor around them. "Look at me!" he demanded, the words lashing out like whips of sound amid the duel battle. "See what your ambition has wrought!"

There was no joy in Rayburn's heart as he pressed his advantage, no satisfaction in the slow creep of desperation that tinged Janus' countenance. Instead, there was only the bitter taste of inevitability, the acknowledgement that this confrontation was the result of a path long since set into motion.

Janus seemed smaller amidst the surge of dark magic. His will faltering in front of his son. He had set out to realize his cause, the victory over the Blindspot, with that achieved his heart searched for a reason to fight on.

Tomoe made her challenge swift; the acolytes lay on the ground covered in their own blood. The Knights had suffered physically from the ritual, their power not even half of what Tomoe expected. The only thing for her to do was to witness the battle of will unfolding before her eyes.

The unshakable confidence that had always defined Janus faltered, giving way to a dawning realization of his impending defeat. Time seemed to dilate, stretching the moment into an eternity as the spell collided with its target. The impact thundered Janus' body was thrown backward, his silhouette etched against the backdrop of chaos like a marionette severed from its strings. He crumpled to the ground, his armor no match for the relentless assault of shadowy tendrils that danced around him in a celebration of victory.

In the stillness that followed, the gravity of what had transpired settled onto Rayburn's shoulders like a mantle woven from the dusk itself. And as he looked upon the broken man at his feet, Rayburn could not help but wonder whether the victory was worth the price paid, or if the darkness within him had exacted a toll too steep to truly measure.

Janus Gravestone's breaths came in ragged gasps as he lay defeated on the bloodstained earth. The once indomitable commander of the Magus Knights, a man whose very name had echoed like thunder through the halls of Sanctamonium, now found himself at the mercy of fate and the hands of his adopted son, Rayburn Wilder.

In those fleeting moments, the labyrinth of Janus' mind unraveled, each thread pulling him back to a time when love had not yet been overshadowed by the specters of vengeance and hatred. Memories, once cherished, now tormented him—the laughter of a child he had come to call his own, the pride that swelled in his chest with every one of Rayburn's achievements. How had his heart become so ensnared by the blind pursuit of power?

He sought out Rayburn's gaze, seeking a glimmer of the bond they once shared, a sign of the affection that had warmed their days. But all he saw reflected back at him was the cold, hard glare of hatred—a mirror to the nightmare his life had spiraled into. A single tear escaped, carving a path through the grime and blood upon his cheek, an eloquent testament to the human soul's capacity for both immense love and ruinous folly.

As the final shroud of life prepared to claim him, Janus' world narrowed to nothing but the sound of his own heartbeat, slowing, faltering—then stopping altogether. His body crumpled, surrendering at last to the silence that awaited him.

Raymond just stood there, his eyes blank, reflecting the blankness in the eyes of Janus. Tomoe, his closest confidant, approached him, her hand reaching out tentatively before settling upon his shoulder. Her eyes wide with empathy, searched his face, trying to fathom the depths of what he had endured, what he had sacrificed.

"Ray," she whispered, her voice a soft undercurrent against the residual clamor of dispersing combatants. "It's over." As Rayburn fell to his knees, the storm within him subsided. Tomoe knelt beside him embracing him; it was her soft touch that was able to calm his nerves. He held her tightly; his emotions overflowing breaking the boundaries he had built within himself. As wallows of cries filled the air, the two became one, their bodies intertwined, and their hearts beats synchronized.

It was to be secret to be held within their hearts. Janus was to be celebrated as the Hero, his death an outcome of his battle against the Sin, the Darkseith Leader; the sacrifices of the Acolytes in defense of the great man.

The sky, once an oppressive canvas of black, began to fray at its seams, allowing the timid caress of dawn to filter through. Rayburn's eyes lifted to the horizon, where the Blindspot had been—a void that had consumed all hope—and now lay bare, exposed to the purifying scrutiny of the rising sun. In this moment of quiet reflection, the weight of silence bore down on him, a counterbalance to the chaos that had raged not long ago. As the first rays of the new dawn stretched across the battlefield, touching the faces of the weary and the wounded, a sense of hope, fragile yet unyielding began to weave itself into the fabric of the morning.

And there, in the embrace of Tomoe and at the boundary of a world teetering between ruin and rebirth, Rayburn Wilder felt the stirrings of possibility. Perhaps it was not too late for redemption; perhaps the very darkness that he harbored could be reshaped into a beacon for those lost amidst the shadows. In the soft glow of the nascent day, Rayburn dared to believe that even the most tarnished soul could find its way back to the light.

The smoldering ruins of the battlefield lay strewn around Sanctamonium, the charred remnants of the Darkseiths still releasing tendrils of smoke into the early dawn. Citizens, their faces gaunt with years of dread and conflict, now stood on the threshold of the Blindspot, eyes wide with a mixture of hope and awe. For the first time in a millennium, the veil had been lifted, revealing to them a world long thought lost to the annals of myth.

"Behold," Seraphim announced, voice cutting clear across the murmurs, "our new dawn."

As if summoned by his words, the sunlight crested the dunes, setting the vast expanse of the desert ablaze with golden hues. The citizens of Sanctamonium stepped forward, hesitant yet drawn to the spectacle. The light was almost physical in its presence, washing over them with warmth, banishing the omnipresent gloom they had resigned themselves to for generations.

"Beautiful," whispered Leandra Skylark, her emerald eyes danced with reflections of the sand's luminance.

Rayburn Wilder remained a silent sentinel at Seraphim's side, dark eyes unblinking as they scanned the landscape. Tomoe allowed herself a small smile; here was proof that their struggle was not in vain.

Together, the group of guardians stood as the embodiment of the light that had triumphed over darkness. The citizens, once shackled by fear, now took their first steps toward the sands, embracing the radiance that beckoned them towards an uncertain but undeniably brighter future.

Chapter 16

The Light beyond the Darkness

In the aftermath, the air hung heavy with an acrid tang of magic spent and lives lost. Dust swirled around Satori as he stepped over the rubble. His posture never wavered, for he carried within him the burden of leadership and the unspoken oath to rebuild from the ashes.

Seraphim waded through the remnants of Sanctamonium, his keen eyes sharply observing the citizens rallying to reclaim their shattered domain. They formed chains, passing broken bricks and splintered beams with a rhythm born of necessity, their movements synchronized by a shared resolve. Dust cloaked their figures, painting them as living statues dedicated to the city's resurrection. Fatigue never seemed to touch them, as they rallied together to rebuild their home. They had witnessed destruction before but the hope of a new future filled them with a light they never before witnessed. The call to arms by Janus had left its mark, with the crumbling Blindspot, the divides between the masses seems to crumble away as well; each trying their best to pitch in to the efforts, to rebuild what was rightfully theirs.

"Careful with that wall!" a voice rang out, its commanding timbre slicing through the clamor.

Volunteers, like a swarm of industrious bees, bustled among the ruins. They carried wooden crates brimming with coins now serving a more urgent purpose than mere trade. These were the sinews of survival—food, water, and medical supplies distributed to hands that trembled not with greed, but gratitude.

The ever present sound of bell tower rang far, the constant in all the turmoil and triumphs, each beat at perfect intervals.......

The new land a desert reflecting the sunlight lay bare in front of the Sanctamonium, like a blank canvas waiting for stories to be written.

On the distant horizon, tranquility slowly began to crumble as chaos seeped in. It was as if unseen forces were forging new paths and a fresh story was about to unfold. The once desolate and neglected land now pulsed with potential, taking on new form and purpose. Mountains rose up from the dusty ground, forests sprouted from the barren soil, and streams trickled through the previously lifeless terrain. Nature's canvas was being painted anew, ready for a new chapter.

EPILOGUE

The Blind Spot was a name that would haunt the city of Sanctamonium for generations to come. The place where the darkness had originated; the epicenter of the plague that had nearly consumed them all. It would take years to rebuild the city and even longer to heal the wounds in the hearts of those who had endured the nightmare.

But rebuild they would, for the people of Sanctamonium were a resilient lot, united by their shared experience. And in the hearts of those who had fought against the darkness, a newfound determination burned brightly.

Together, they vowed, they would ensure that nothing like this would ever happen again. They would stand vigilant against the encroaching shadows, ready to face whatever nightmares the future might bring.

For they were the mages of Sanctamonium and they had stared into the face of the abyss...

And they had won.

Avalone, the forgotten city, lay untouched by the chaos that had recently consumed Sanctamonium. Within its tallest tower, beneath the vast dome painted with constellations, the Council convened in urgent whispers.

It was then that the grand doors of the council hall burst open with a thunderous echo. Cloaked in darkness, a messenger entered, his presence slicing through the charged atmosphere like a blade through silence. Every head turned as he advanced, sweeping towards the heart of the room where the council sat.

"The Divide has been breached," his voice resonated, cutting short the murmurs of the assembly. The words hung ominously, a somber shroud descending upon the mages.

His pale hands emerged from the folds of his cloak, gesturing with urgency. "The Darkseiths' have been defeat and the Divide conquered." The council members nodded, the gravity of the situation etched on their faces. Each understood the peril that lay beyond the safety of their enchanted walls. For centuries, the Divide had shielded them, now its rupture threatened to unravel the fabric of their world.

"Prepare the emissaries," The council ordered.

www.ingramcontent.com/pod-product-compliance
Lightning Source LLC
LaVergne TN
LVHW041608070526
838199LV00052B/3038